Buster

Buster

Alan Burns

CALDER

CALDER PUBLICATIONS
an imprint of

ALMA BOOKS LTD
3 Castle Yard
Richmond
Surrey TW10 6TF
United Kingdom
www.calderpublications.com

Buster first published by John Calder (Publishers) Ltd in 1961
This edition first published by Calder Publications in 2019

Text © Alan Burns, 1961, 2019

Cover design by Will Dady

Printed and bound by CPI Group (UK) Ltd, Croydon, CR0 4YY

ISBN: 978-0-7145-4920-0

Contents

Buster

Buster:

A small new loaf or large bun
A thing of superior size or astounding nature
A burglar
A spree
A dashing fellow
A Southerly gale with sand or dust
A piece of bread and butter
A very successful day
Hollow, utterly, low
To fall or be thrown

(DICTIONARIES)

Chapter 1

T HEY STOOD OVER HIM.
Grandma shrieked:
"Let me look at you! What a big boy you've grown!
Have a chocolate! Have a pear! Have some more seed-
cake, darling! You're not eating anything! How can
you be a big man without eating anything? What is he
going to be when he grows up?"
"Lord Chief Justice," said his father.
"Prime Minister," said Grandma. "Danny, who do you
like better – your mother or your father?"
"Both the same," he said.

That night he wrapped the sheets round it, then a
mountain of blankets, then the eiderdown tucked in.
Small pig hot inside. Then wet.

In the bath his mother had told him never play with
that. Never. It's dirty. It will make you go mad, like
being bitten by a frothy dog. Told him again and
again how his cousin had stood up to make himself

soapy, but his heel felt the curve of the bath and his spine cracked the edge of the bath and the nerve was crushed and the bone splintered and the track for the nerve from the brain to the legs was ruined and he sits in a chair all day now. Dan had seen those legs in their grey flannel trousers, skinny knees poking through like pins.

But this was so easy and lovely. He watched moonlit clouds slide evenly between him and the moon.

His mother's hand held his hand, pointed at the sheets. His face pushed into the smelly sheets.

"You wait till your father comes home. You just wait."

She had locked the dining-room door. He walked slowly round the table, squeaking his fingers on the polished wood; he slid his penknife along the grooves, collected threads of dirt. He stood on the window sill, looked out over the hedge into the road. A soldier posted a letter. He jumped onto the couch; his feet sank in as he pranced about on it. He waited. He reached up for the sweet dish; it fell on the carpet. Liquorice allsorts. He crawled round picking them up: one for the dish, one for his mouth. He poked under the tails of the green monkeys climbing the vase; when they reached the top he'd get a Rolls Royce. He sat on the couch and waited.

He saw the car through the window. Quickly he put his father's slippers in front of the big chair. It was his job. He banged on the door.

"Let me out!"

He wanted to be first, to run down the path, be swung up onto the garden wall, given a piggyback. The door stayed shut. He heard them talking. He kicked the slippers across the room. They lay in the empty fireplace. They were black-and-red tartan wool.

Upstairs to the spare room, his father treading behind. He pulled his trousers down; they wouldn't come over his shoes.

"That's enough!"

He hobbled to the bed, lay across it. The prickles of the hairbrush touched his bottom.

"Get up and get dressed. You'll go straight to bed without supper."

He heard them arguing. His mother brought him snap crackle pop with milk.

He heard his brother coming up the stairs. He bounced up and down, making the bedsprings prink. Bryan came in, sat on the bed, smiled, waited.

"I hate her," Dan said.

"You shouldn't. She's your mother."

"She's got sticking-out eyes and frizzy hair."

"That's only because she's not got enough iodine."

There was an old brown photo of her kissing under an orange tree.

"I'm a cruiser with six-inch guns," Bryan said, "and father's a battleship and mother's the Ark Royal, stuffed with tuck instead of planes."

"What about me?"

"Oh, you're nothing. You don't want to be in this fleet."

"I do."

"Well, you're a brilliant destroyer – the fastest ship in the navy. And you've got torpedoes which can sink anything."

"Where are we going?"

"We're steaming across the Bay of Biscay to fight for Spain."

"Then what happens?"

"Tell you tomorrow. Go to sleep."

"Now."

"Tomorrow. Goodnight, sleep well."

"Goodnight. I don't want to be Lord Chief Justice."

"You haven't got to be."

"They all say I will."

"Never mind them. Goodnight, whippersnapper."

"Night."

Chapter 2

B RYAN WAS HOME ALL DAY, because he had finished school and not found a job yet. They played French cricket in the garden, and read a story in *The Wizard* about U-boats, and Dan made a speech in Parliament:

"Why should the rich have pears and cake and the poor can't even have bread?"

Bryan said: "Hooray!"

Boys came round, and they held Dan between them and raced him along the street, flying him into the air. "Let me down! Let me down!"

But when they stopped, he cried: "Do it again!"

"Come in and listen to the wireless. Sh! It's important."

Mr Chamberlain.* The war had started. The air-raid siren went. Dan got under the dining-room table. His mother was making tea; she bent down and looked in:

"You all right down there?"

He hugged the crosspiece between his legs. He was nine. They were talking about boarding school.

His father said: "It's too much for you, dear. Bryan can look after himself. But the other one…"

His father stood at the foot of the bed:

"I'm sorry, Dan. It's the war. We didn't know there was going to be a war, did we?"

"Here's a pound for spends," his father was shouting as the train moved off.

"What?"

"Not 'what' – pardon. Look after your mother and write every week."

Staring out of the train windows. Boring. Just fields. Reading *Woman* and *Melody Maker* with mother.

Strange roads. Greygravel path. Grey walls. Eyesocket staring windows. Standing while mother mumbled with Headmaster. Unbroken tradition. Evacuated. Discipline. Horse-riding and Music extra. Tall boy walked slowly past the open door, twisting his head to stare. Matron. Cash's name tapes. Down a corridor, clicking a radiator. Mother grabbed his arm. Corridors leading off. Hundreds of doors. He would never find his way around.

"He will have to be inspected."

Trousers down round his ankles, getting creased. Hobbling, taking the fawn rug with him over the slidy floor. Mother getting up to help.

Doctor roaring: "He'd better get used to undressing himself!"

The carefully balanced timetable cut up the days. Mr Hoffman took Geography. Two sweets after lunch followed by compulsory rest period. Miss Lazarus took French. Desks in rows. Mr Hoffman walked up and down; sometimes he was in front, sometimes behind your back. Miss Lazarus had a special high desk she had bought herself in France. Diagrams on the walls. A woman cut through the middle; green kidneys, orange heart. A fat minim, black crotchets, quavers, semiquavers, demisemiquavers. The British Empire rolled down red, and on a dusty table in the corner a relief map of the neighbourhood with cardboard roads and bits of green sponge trees.

He stood on the cold, bumpy football field, by the white goalposts. The others charged around. If only he could dribble right through them and smash the ball into the net... But he was glad he wasn't one of those who just ran near the ball, shouting, pretending.

Mr Beezley made Dan Sweeping Prefect, and in front of everybody showed him how to hold the broom so as not to sweep the dust onto his own shoes. Mr Beezley took Latin. O table. Smack smack smack smack. Dan's eyes went flat on four walls.

Anything could happen on Sunday. He walked through the garden at the back; looked into the greenhouse at the black grapes dangling in bubbled bunches from the green vine spreading out. Over the fence, scratched by rusty wire, down the middle of the road past the chestnut tree with the cobbled wall round it, into a wood he'd never been in before.

He sensed the deep heat of autumn, saw it gobbling up the green, scraped thick moss onto his hand. Out into a new wide field, hunting for mushrooms. Hand down in wetness, fingers at the base of the stalk, gentle snap, then peel back a strip of skin to make sure it wasn't a toadstool, nibble a bit. Puffball – puff, brown smoke. He pocketed hazelnuts. He wrenched a stick from the hedge and swiped the hedge with it. He struck the neck of a drooping flower; the dark head slipped off and down into damp dark grass. The split stalk shivered, showed sticky white blood. A tremble fixed his hand, held his stomach, legs, head. Stock-still unbelief. A hawk hovered. He pointed his stick straight at the one-pin dangerous eye. At school he was bumped awake. He told them about the fox he had seen close up.

Harry Finegold made him go horse-riding. Such tough necks. Dan was too skinny. When the horse chewed grass, shoving his neck down, he couldn't pull him up. Harry Finegold gripped with his knees, got the horse between his legs. Dan sat on top. He trotted, bumping. The horse saw home a half-mile down the road; his back hooves slipped as he jerked forwards in a sudden gallop. Dan sat straight as a Bengal Lancer. He could not believe he was galloping. Then slowly he slipped sideways.

"Up you get!"

Harry's voice: "No."

"You're going to be Prime Minister and you can't even ride a pony!"

He dreamt he was searching for someone among shopping crowds. He caught up with her; she changed; he saw her farther on. He held her sleeve; it came away; it was a German; black-clad Germans swung from parachutes; columns of Germans with rifles marched over him. He clung to a bomber's wings, diving into trees, rocketing up, looping through the clouds. And at night he found easier, suppler ways – unobtrusive sexy ways. That lovely feel of between, squeezed between his slippery thighs, or under him. And in the garden lavatory, wooden bucket seat, stinking pail, he found old soft sweets, covered himself with them.

He worked at the piano. He held his hands and wrists correctly, tapped each note separate and clear. All Sunday he practised the first page of his piece.

"Quite good. A little wooden. Go on."

"That's all I've done."

"Better play it right through, even badly."

"What's the use of playing badly? I want to play it brilliantly, perfectly, better than anyone else has ever played it."

At half-term he gave up the piano.

The headmaster took General Knowledge. He explained about clocks, Parliament, motor cars, the armed forces, icebergs, telephones, pollination, traffic lights, Mount Everest expeditions, orchestras, railway engines. It was Dan's best subject. For his task he gave a talk on the Russian Revolution, and made a coloured map to show the dispositions of the Interventionist armies. At home, when his report came, his father was proud of the second in General Knowledge, and told Grandma and Uncle George. That his position in form was twelfth out of fifteen was only because he hadn't settled down yet.

At home Dan missed the countryside, and he walked often in the park. He would whistle 'The Trumpet Voluntary' or 'The Blue Danube' as loudly and perfectly as he could. Perhaps a composer or a violinist would come up and say: "You whistle very beautifully, young man. You have an exceptionally sensitive ear. You must take up music – one day you will be great." Or he sang 'The Marseillaise', hoping that a Frenchman would recognize it and reward him for loyalty to the Republic.*

Bryan one morning marched off to the park to help dig trenches and fill sandbags. He held a garden spade rifle-wise and did a "P-r-e-s-e-n-t arms!" Dan went to watch. At lunchtime they sat together on a park seat. Bryan tried to rub the clay off his flannels. "You're the first to know, Dan. I'm joining the army."

"God! Dad won't let you."

"I must—"

"But Dad says you're doing war work."

"As his secretary! Any woman could do the job. I'm nothing. I didn't even go to Spain."

"You weren't old enough."

"It's the same war, and I'm old enough now."

"I'm going too."

"You stay at school and work like mad. You're the clever one. You've got a big chance."

Dan wandered round the park, and arrived back at the trenches to go home with his brother. They walked along without speaking. Dan was annoyed: "Why don't you say anything?"

"I'm thinking. And I'm tired."

"But I love having proper conversations with you."

"You can't order 'one conversation' like a pound of apples."

"You talk with Philip all the time."

"We exchange ideas."

Dan was silent. Then, near home, he said: "Plato did all the talking, and the others just said 'Oh yes' or 'I don't agree' to set him off again. I could do that with you."

Bryan said: "Okay. You win. But it's a bit late now."

"Yes. But after the war."

"Of course."

Bryan spoke quietly, coolly, explaining. His mother sobbed: "You mustn't go – you'll get killed; don't go, please, for my sake." His father said: "Why didn't you discuss it with me first? But we understand how you feel. You must do what you think is right." Dan listened.

Bryan's training camp was "somewhere in Scotland". Dan watched him go on the nameless express. The thread linking their eyes pulled and pulled and snapped. Dan sat with his arms folded. An iron shovel shovelled bricks behind a planked wall of advertisements. Above, dirty panes of tough glass backed by steel netting shut off the sky. On the wide platform people walked in various directions, away from each other, unconnected, yet together making a pattern. Clip clink tread pad in time with tinned music from loudspeakers. Fat pigeons walked among them, heads bobbing out of time with their feet. An unprepared roar and shriek of steam frightened the young ones, made them jump and fly a few yards. The people took no notice. A little boy was dragged along by his mother as she hurried off somewhere; his spare hand wiped his runny nose. Three young soldiers, sweating in thick uniform, drifted by, grinning. Whippersnappers raced in and out of telephone boxes, pressing button B. Nuns looked funny and young in light blue, their big white hats turned up like paper gliders. They chatted and nodded. An Irish voice: "It was a wedding present. He picked it out with a pin." Two girls in sky-blue shorts were glared at. *I Speak Your Weight* spoke a lady's *Fourteen Stone Four Pounds* to everyone as she giggled. Sticks dropped and bounced on the platform. Porters shoved trolleys loaded with cartons of kippers Deposit Four Shillings. A girl from India stood blinding in orange. The fruit stall was a box on the platform, a spare bit in the train set. A pound of apples, paid for, was left on the counter. A face looked out, then a hand took the bag inside. Men wandered into the Gents' Hairdressing & Brush-Up, emerged unchanged. A tramp searched for fag ends;

his head was twisted so that his cheek was forced permanently against his shoulder. Ticket collector touched the hands of girls and watched them onto the train. Yorkshireman talked extra loud in London. A kid swung on his father's hand: Father smiled wide and lovely. People walked in various directions, away from each other – unconnected, yet together making a pattern.

He took the war map from Bryan's room to his own. He replaced the little flags on pins which marked the positions of the armies: union jacks, tricolours, swastikas. He stretched coloured cotton across the pins to mark the Maginot and Siegfried lines. He cut out a big flag, marked it with a red "B" and stuck it in Scotland.

Bryan sent letters to his brother at school, and in the holidays enclosed a separate note for him in the family letter. Once he mentioned that on his first leave he would "sell a lot of old junk, including my bicycle". Dan hauled the bicycle out of the garage, mended the punctures, cleaned the chromium. He looked through the "wanted" columns of the local newspapers, cycled miles around reading cards in newsagents' windows, and in the end sold it for six pounds, which he kept in his brother's room. Another letter advised Dan to:

"Do some proper reading. Less newspapers and politics. You're old enough to read the classics. Only real learning counts." Dan took *War and Peace* from his father's bookcase and read it in five weeks.

He talked about Pierre,* who proved his philosophy by algebra. In each letter Bryan told him to work hard and look after his mother.

Bryan came home on leave and told them he had been posted to India. He tied a knot in the corner of his handkerchief and danced it round the table, like a raja with a turban. "It takes more than a world war to get you down," his father said.
"When I die put three hundredweight of marble on my grave, and inscribe it: 'LAUGH THIS ONE OFF'," Bryan replied.

At school Dan tried to study, had few friends, rarely wrote home. Each term he won the form prize for poetry speaking. He enjoyed standing alone on the broad stage, pronouncing the words of poems perfectly, making his voice break with emotion. He received his prize to a patter of clapping.

In the holidays there were air raids. An oil bomb dropped on the park. It seemed more real than other bombs: a tank of oil falling from up there onto the ground. Oil seemed heavier than steel. A morning bomb shattered the bathroom windows, covering the floor with powdery glass. His mother screamed and wept: "Your father always shaves at eight o'clock, and today he didn't. Thank God. Thank God. There is a God, after all!"

Dan helped her sweep up the glass; she held the newspaper while he swept the glass onto it. The monkey vase had got broken, so he went out for some Seccotine.*

Where the corner newsagent had been still smelt of charred wood and dusty rubble. He wondered about the paper bill.

At home his mother called from the kitchen: "Mend it in here, Danny, and keep me company. And put some newspaper on the table so the glue won't make so much mess."

"It will make the same mess, but it won't matter so much," he said.

He popped the monkeys into the vase and said he'd like his Rolls Royce with grey Hooper coachwork.* The cat got a piece of paper glued to his fur, and raced round the kitchen, chased by the paper. They laughed, and she hugged him till he had to push away to breathe, still laughing.

One morning, very early, he started off to cycle into the country. He heard his mother running after him. "Wait, Danny. I'll walk with you a little way. I'm taking some cheesecake over to Dolly's. Jack's not well."

He called back: "I must get to Hertford by lunchtime." But he waited for her, and they went along together, she holding the handlebar while he rocked his feet against the pedals. He wobbled over the road. "I must get on," he said, impatient.

He heard the hum of a plane.

"Please leave, go."

Heavy sound of the plane, throbbing. Gurrum-gurrumgurrumgurrum loudsoft loudsoft loudsoft a heart. He was fifty yards down the street when the noise stopped and the thought flashed "Buzzbomb". Roar and boom into his eyes. The front wheel yanked sideways. He felt his elbow slithering against asphalt. His sleeve filled with blood. He ran to his mother. She lay on her back, stretched out as he had seen her sunbathing in the garden. Only her foot seemed twisted. The weight of that foot on the ground. The brown-leather shoe, lace pulled tight and neat, double bow tied precisely. The leather had the glow that comes from unthinking morning polishing over years, brown turning to black with work. The force of the blow against the asphalt road had torn open the outer leather in one place, exposing its yellow inside like the slit belly of a pus-filled pig.

A policeman wrote in his notebook: "Scratch on left shoe approx one inch". The foot had a slight unnatural twist at the ankle. She could not have bent her foot like that if she had been alive. The difference was small – an angle of ten degrees. But alive she could not have done it without breaking the bone, gouging one bone into the other, wrenching the muscle enough to make her scream with pain or come as near to screaming as an ill middle-aged woman can – not a young clean scream, but a choke, a sob, a cough, a constriction in the throat caused by too much trying to escape at one time. Weight is being drawn into the earth, pulled to the middle of it. Her foot weighed.

"She's bought it," the policeman said.

He dragged the body into a doorway beside a butcher's shop. He bawled up a steep flight of stairs: "Someone give us a 'and?"

A man came downstairs. He unlocked a door into the shop and helped carry the body inside. Dan could see them standing up in the shop, the body between them on the sawdust floor. They took no notice of him. He ran up the stairs and stood on the unfamiliar landing. A door was partly open, and through the E-shaped gap he saw a woman in a yellow electric-lit room. She wore a yellow flowered dressing gown. She was kneeling in front of a fireplace, trying to pull the string from a bundle of firewood. It caught on splinters. She poked one stick through, then another, then two or three at a time until the whole bundle collapsed. She threw the sticks on crumpled newspaper. She added small coal to the pile, then put a match to it. She dropped the string on the flames.

He was freewheeling downhill homewards. He had ridden into the country, as far as Hertford. Smoke rose straight from the chimney. Through the windows he saw his father playing chess.

He stood in the dining room, waiting for the solemn talk. He looked at her empty chair, remembered seeing her white bottom once when he'd gone into their bedroom without knocking.

He was taken upstairs to the spare room. He had stationed hundreds of lead soldiers over the floor, flicked marbles at them. An unused bookcase held

Bryan's old books – Left Book Club, Thinker's Library.* He tried to cry.

"You'd better go back to school. It would be best."

"But it's the holidays. There'll be no one there."

"Never mind. We'll ring them up."

From the country railway station he cycled to school: through the village, along a muddy lane, bumping down into puddled hollows, watching the marks of tyres in thin mud. The camouflaged waterworks crawled with yellow monsters. His head felt queer, like blotting paper. He stopped. He looked up at the flat sky. It was empty except for those specks floating past his eyes, which he knew were caused by minute particles slipping between the retina and the iris and slowly easing down.

That term he missed the big food parcels from home. So he stole from the food cupboard: he slid back the brown door just a few inches, pushed his hand inside and picked up whatever was nearest – a bar of chocolate, a tin of sardines.

He was senior enough to have a study. He shared with Michael – a smooth-faced neat boy whose father was a Member of Parliament. Michael was to enter politics.

"I think my first step will be to obtain a position in local government," he told Dan.

"A job with the Council? I wouldn't do that."

"Why?"

"Haven't you seen that notice on their carts? It reads: 'Gratuities forbidden'. I'd like a job where you can make something on the side."

Michael talked about his family – proudly of his father, glowingly of his sister. Dan was invited to Sunday lunch. The father gave him orangeade and remarked that the weather was pretty frightful for cricket. Dan said that today was not good, but it was better than yesterday. The day before had been perhaps a little better than yesterday, but not quite so good as today. Tomorrow the position would be complicated still further, and the day after that the complexity would become unbearable. Suicide, and an eternity of good (or bad) days, seemed the only solution. Michael got the biggest helpings of roast beef; his sister was tall and wore thick stockings. Over lunch Dan talked about incest and the Oedipus complex.

Michael used the study less often. Dan enjoyed being alone. He ate fingerfuls of Radio Malt.* He looked up words in the dictionary. Rape is an administrative division of Surrey. He began to write an epic poem. He borrowed his brother's typewriter. His father sent him a ream of foolscap typing paper. Dan typed on the first sheet a word: "Onion". And then, brilliantly: "Man. Onion Man". What a picture! Was there another mind in the school that could have conceived it? In the whole county of Gloucestershire, in England, Europe, the Universe? Time was grander. Multiply together all the billions of minds and moments there had ever been – had one once deliberately and self-consciously thought: Onion Man? Pause. Knowledge. How many

men there were whose life was onions, whose sons
had onion seller owner eater dealer digger dads.
Uniqueness demanded disjointedness. Irrelevance
was the key. To onion add the word least like onion...

He was picked for the house chess team, and decided
to become a professional. His father sent him untidy
parcels of books by Lasker and Capablanca,* and
he swotted the first chapters. He played chess with
Montague, who had been brought up in Chicago and
Paris, had a motorbike, girlfriends, cigars, coloured
waistcoats and a thousand gramophone records,
which he and Dan listened to on sports afternoons.
They conversed about composers.

Of course the move from Beethoven to Brahms
reflected the growing complexity of the contradic-
tions inherent in capitalist society," said Dan.
"Say, bud, you don't say so!" Montague replied.
"Yeah, Clodface, I do say so."

The music formed a background to Dan's thoughts
about himself.

They played word games.
"Describe midsummer in terms of sound," Montague
said.
"Beethoven's Ninth performed by an orchestra with
ten million first violins and the Massed Choirs of
the Universe. And midwinter?"
"The sound made when T.S. Eliot taps his teeth with
his spectacles."

They discussed genius. Was Dan a genius?
"You're obsessed with the word," Montague said.

"But what does it mean?"

"Genius is another name for pride," said his friend, "and pride is the cardinal virtue."

"Genius is the ability to achieve extraordinary things," said Dan.

"No, it is the achievement, by work, of extraordinary things. For example, could you spend the entire week at school, saying only 'fish paste'?"

"I am unique and I will amaze people," said Dan.

"Unique? That's very ordinary. And who fails to amaze their mo— father?" his friend asked.

"Aren't you a genius?"

"You mean will I exchange recognition? I'm afraid not. You remain the supplicant."

Soon after he was made a prefect, Dan walked into Montague's form room:

"You're making a shocking noise. This is a sixth form and should be an example to the others."

They looked at him, silent. Montague was smiling.

"And don't smile when you are being admonished."

As he left he heard his friend's French-American drawl: "*Quel sang froid! Quel savoir-faire!*"*

The boy bent over correctly and touched his toes. The skin on his bare legs and buttocks stretched tight. He was trembling.

"The other way," Dan said.

The boy straightened a little, touched the edge of the washstand with his hands. He was thirteen. At the daily "hands inspection" he had been caught three times with dirty fingernails. The traditional punishment was a caning by the duty prefect. Dan wanted to thrash him. He was beautiful, and Dan wanted to hurt and bruise him. He let the cane touch the boy's skin.

"Get to bed. You're lucky this time."

Dan was reprimanded. He said he could not support capital punishment – no, he meant corporal punishment. The dignity of man, Tom Paine,* scientific humanism, principles. His prefect's tie, red with a gold stripe, was formally taken away from him at a special ceremony in the prefects' common room.

"You have precisely one hour left, gentlemen." The invigilator's plummy voice, artificial as a bishop's, sounded through the examination hall. Dan's school-leaving certificate: English Literature. The main question read: "Dr Johnson was the Hero of his Age. Discuss."

Dan wrote:

Johnson in the Modern Eye*

Johnson was god. And typical of his age. Era of Goodsense worship, sameness the ultimate ideal, piggery and prudery rife, nonsense wisdom, pomposity prestige.

So the Nightmareman Must – mountain of conventional revulsion, foul-mannered filth loving big boar beast – of course he Must be part of every mantelpiece. A great lumping tasteless victorian grandfather clock, stumpgomping on top of and right through the pretty coffee cups and sniki simplicities. How he bounds! And Boswell is his weak-tea shadow And the drawingroom clusters and the Dryden Chandelier and the Johnson and the titters are blushed and the boom begins... he would not like little cracker nuts but with big lumping joll stump off with blugging beaf hunks. And guzzle. And cover his ear with gravy. And guffaw. And stuck his feet and glush his mouth the modern dainty mind reflects recedes back back

But now when the cooling stonily creeps me and I can see him just plain big, not glumping, clumsy yes but his thud was live and he jollily glowed in thrilling proudness of town and culture and coffee house fine conversation and rightness (who will read it?) of the good occasion and the truth

And he warms his behind by the redfire large and lust and he glows. His great brown pipe I can see in his great brown fist and his boots. Gleaming black and sturdy. The socks must be wool (hand woven quite good) and the lack of a bath quite foul. I'm here and I'm now away from the stench feast and the big fug   for I'm modern and fine young man.

"Idiot!" Montague said. "They'll fail you."

Dan knew it. He felt sick.

"I won't fail. I don't care if I fail. I'll show them. I won't join the army. I won't get a job. I won't queue. I'd rather walk. I'll go to London. I'll get a girl and go up west. She'll curve and have a curvy dress. I'll jive with her. I'll sling her round the room. I'll pull her between my legs. She'll be jumping mad. I'll kiss her cheeks. I'll slap her bum till it stings. I'll burn her name on my arm. I'll sleep with her. I'll sleep in the park. I'll get soaked. I'll march. Hope it pours. Hope we get soaked and drenched and drowned. I'll have a long wet crazy beard. I'll slosh through the gutters. I'll smash their windows. I'll yell. I'll knife you. I'm going up west. Coming? We're dead tomorrow."

"I'm not coming," Montague said.

Chapter 3

PLANK FROM COLLAR TO BUM. Head back, eyes set, chin in, shoulders back, tummy in, bottom in, legs straight, heels together, feet at an angle of forty-five degrees, thumbs stretched down the seams of the trousers. Cap band polished, best serge pressed and creased to cut, webbing belt and straps tight, clean and tough, pack emptied, cut square and plywood-stiffened, slices of brass set slick as a flick knife, polished to whiteness. Cap, collar, pack, each precisely parallel to concrete slabs beneath the boots. Boots. Eyeblinding, scintillating brilliant boots.

The cartoon brigadier treads slowly by, unbelievably moustachioed, inspecting.

"Completed basic training?"

"Sir!"

"Category?"

"Clerk. General duties. Sir!"

"Enjoying the army?"

"Sir!"

Behind, walls of dirt. Deadgrey walls, dirt colour. Narrow jail windows. The plaster, hard and flaky with age, crumbles: at a touch powdered wall snows on the scrubbed wood floor. Rifles will not be leant against walls.

Condemned as uninhabitable each year since 1905, Talavera Barracks were most suitable for the accommodation of national servicemen during basic training.

"Carry on, Sergeant Major."

"D-i-i-i-is-miss!"

A thousand men swivel right on the right heel, bring left leg up till thigh is parallel to the ground: crunching crash as a thousand boots slam down.

The men grumbled across the parade ground. They went to the NAAFI,* queued for tea, strained forwards to see the cakes and bacon sandwiches and Irish girls and sausage and mash. The food was served on Bakelite plates by girls in sexless overalls.

The Church of England hall had dusty lampshades and cobwebs on the walls, and you were served by old ladies in floral dresses and hairnets and spectacles. On Tuesdays the NAAFI had cod and chips and the C of E was empty. As usual the ladies apologized for not having "frying facilities".

"We've applied so often, but there isn't the money today."

Though tonight was cod night, Dan preferred to sit alone in the C of E with *Titbits* and a cup of tea. He had just heard that the NAAFI put something in the tea "to make you sleep well".

"I don't like being done good to on the sly," he said.

He worried about his rifle. The bolt was missing. How could it have happened? Bayonet practice tomorrow. Bound to be rifle inspection. And some idiot had kicked his toecap on parade. Need a good two hours' work to get it right again. They said burning the leather with a hot iron gave a smooth surface that polished up beautifully. It was a gamble. Perhaps it would ruin them. That bolt. "Pull bolt back for inspection of magazine." Had he failed to "ram bolt securely home" so that it had slipped back onto the ground? He left the canteen quickly and ran to the parade ground. He tried to find the spot where his section had been having rifle instruction. It was dark. He got down on his knees to look. The smooth-looking concrete was rough and jagged to touch. Like a razor blade under a microscope.

"See a pin, pick it up, and all that day you'll be in the bleedin' shit. What the hell are you doing?"

It was Bert.

"Riding a bloody bicycle. I'm looking for my rifle bolt," said Dan.

"Blimey! It shouldn't happen to me ma-in-law. You'll get ten years jankers!"

"That's why I'm looking for it."

"Bet someone nicked it. Well, be 'ung for a bleedin' sheep. Come onto Parsons Field."

"What for?"

"Apples. Lovely red ruddy apples."

Dan didn't want apples.

"Okay, I'll come."

In the dark they climbed among fruit trees, pushing apples into all their pockets. Bert had brought his kitbag and they saw him heaving it on his shoulders, heard a loud whisper: "I'm off."

Ginger, Dan's partner in latrine fatigues, was mooning about in the shadows. Dan was giving him a leg up a tree when a huge hand thudded on his shoulder. He fell back, Ginger on top of him. Sprawling on the ground they saw standing over them a giant with a shotgun.

"Look at that shotgun," whispered Dan; "he can keep his ruddy daughter."

"None o' your lip."

He was enormous. Dan kept quiet. They were taken into a brightly lit kitchen and stood against the wall "to wait for the military". Sergeant Lewis came:

"You'll be up before the CO* for this."

"Ya yah yah yah yah yah YAAAAAAAAA!" screamed Sergeant Bussel. "That's the way. Yell as you charge. Scare him to death. Hands grip the butt, and UP into his guts. No slashing about the face. UP into his guts. There's no second chances with bayonets. It's him or you. And those Ruskies know a thing or two, I can tell you. Right now. First man."

A man ran at the dummy and prodded it with his bayonet. "Yell!" yelled the Sergeant, "and HATE him! There's no hate in you lads. You don't last long with a bayonet without hating. Next man!"

The dummy on the rope was still moving, and Dan went to steady it before the next man charged. He saw that someone had painted a moustache and spectacles on the face.

Sergeant Bussel shouted like a madman: "What do you think you're doing? Come back here! Now! At the double! Who's in command of this exercise? Who's been running this lot for twenty years? You or me? Who told you to touch the target before the charge? Want to get sliced up? And who'd carry the can back?"

"I thought it should be straight, Sergeant."

"Who told you to think? Would Ivan sit 'straight' while you went up nice and polite and stuck a bayonet in his guts?"

"No, Sergeant."

"Right then. Next man. And YELL."

No rifle inspection. There was a God, after all.

The bolt, wrapped in paper, lay on Dan's bed. On the paper, a word: "Thanks". Dan checked the number, rammed it home, sat on the bed, thinking about apples.

"We're on the board," said Ginger. "CO's Office, 1400 hours."

"Christ," Dan said.

Roaring at them, the Regimental Sergeant Major drove them into the office, marching them in treble-quick time. Bareheaded, they stood stiff at attention, rigid. Across the wide desk the Commanding Officer looked up from a file of papers. "Sergeant Lewis?"

"Sir. At 1700 hours I relieved Sgt. Watkins as Orderly Sergeant—"

The CO snapped: "Where did you find the accused?"

"Sir. I proceeded to the premises, where I found the accused with apples in their possession, which they admitted were not their property. Sir."

"Thank you, Sergeant. You, men, have you anything to say?"

Ginger said: "I didn't know they were private apples, sir. I just saw them and nipped over and nicked them. I thought it was all right, sir. Everybody—"

"Yes, yes. Graveson?"

"I only want to say I am very sorry indeed, sir, for all the trouble I have caused and—"

"Very well. I have carefully considered the facts of this case... Far too much disregard for the property rights of neighbouring landowners... Fine of ten pounds."

"No CB and no fatigues!"* Dan was laughing. "He couldn't wait to get back to his brandy!"

"I'd rather fatigues. It's a ruddy fortune," said Ginger. "It'll be stopped out of your pay. You'll hardly notice it."

"I already send my mum a pound a week, and she keeps saying that's not enough. She thinks I'm made of money."

"A pound a week!"

"I gave her four in Civvy Street.* Now what can I tell her?"

"Write and explain what's happened."

"Tell her there's a thief in the family? She'd never laugh that one off."

"Thief? Still, you can't send her anything for the next ten weeks. Haven't you an uncle who could help?"

Ginger shrugged his shoulders.

"Perhaps I could?..." Dan said.

"Nah."

He walked off, hands in pockets.

Dan wondered how he could pay his own fine. His father's five pounds a month had all gone. He would ask Bryan. He composed a letter. It was difficult. He remembered Bryan's return "after the war". The special troop train. The first glimpse in the crowd of the white shirt, red tie, blue jacket worn by troops in hospital. Bryan had just been reclassified "walking sick". "My biggest thrill in years." The absolute change. Thinning hair, nervous glancing eyes, no concentration. "No wounds, no gallantry in action," he said, "just dreary killing malaria." Bryan sent the ten pounds in a registered envelope, without a message. But the fine was paid – that was the main thing.

Queen's Regulations,* War Office Orders, Army Orders, Standing Orders for Division, Regiment, Battalion. These were all transmitted down to Battalion level. Battalion headquarters was neck-deep in orders. More important, all orders were continually revised and amended. Important for Dan, because he was Orders Clerk. He had scissors and paste. He cut out the new revised version and pasted it over the old. The amendments were specially printed to cover entirely on the page the paragraph they were intended to replace. Dan was instructed to paste the slivers of paper by their edges, so that they could be lifted up and the old order consulted, because certain matters remained governed by the old orders. For example, stores purchased in 1946 would stay governed by the orders of that year; amendments to the Stores Purchasing Orders, therefore, must not be allowed completely to obscure the 1946 orders. Dan became skilled at amending amendments to previously amended orders. And, like all HQ personnel, he was allowed to wear shoes instead of boots and gaiters. He did not have to clean his boots or blanco* his gaiters.

He was waving Queen's Regulations over his desk, the latest amendments, flowing paper tails, looped the loop, flapped backwards and forwards. Captain Ames came in, with a young gunner. The Captain wanted all forms and regulations relating to signing-on in the regular army. "They will be sent to your office, sir."

"No, better do it now."

The Captain pulled two chairs up to Dan's desk, motioning the Gunner forwards. They sat down, and the boy, hunched over his pen, filled in the forms slowly and carefully. His nails were bitten and dirty. Dan could read the black capitals. *Donald MacAndrew. 18 years.* He looked nearer fifteen, had spots on his chin. *Crane driver's assistant. Expresses a desire to join Her Majesty's... Twelve years' engagement.* Typewriters clicked. The boy peered about the office, as if trying to find his way about. The Sergeant nodded and smiled. Captain Ames said:

"Jolly good show."

The boy seemed pleased to have pleased everyone. Dan tried to catch his eye but did not manage to do so.

* * *

"Get up, you lazy bastard!" Bert hurled a pillow against the wall above Dan's head, bringing a shower of plaster down on him.

"You're on the board."

"Not again!"

"It's all right, mate, you're going to be a ruddy officer."

Twelve foot drop. Impossible. Better stay in the ranks for ever. Why did they need an assault course with a twelve-foot jump to distinguish between officer material and the other stuff? The Colonel had talked of "modern methods of officer selection", but this was feudal.

"Hurry along, gentlemen – only thirty-seven seconds to go."

"Gentlemen"! Dan strained for the New World. With a look straight down, he jumped.

The selection-board psychiatrist dropped his handkerchief on the floor, looked up at Dan and said:
"Well?"

"Well what?"

"Talk about what I have just done."

Dan talked, very rapidly: "You have just dropped your handkerchief on the floor. It's a queer thing to do, just like that. It's a dirtyish floor, but your handkerchief is fairly clean, so apparently you don't drop it often. It was queer because it was disjointed it bore – or seemed to bear – no relation to what had gone before. That is unusual in a human action. The causal relationship between successive actions is usually apparent. Which sounds clever, but is, in fact, a platitude. No, it is profound and also untrue. My confusion results from my avoiding complex subjects like free will and determinism, which are the roots of the question. Things drop with varying velocities, depending on their weight. No, the velocity is constant. I think it called G_2, but I don't know what G_2 is—"

"That will do. You may go now. Thank you."

As Dan went to the door, the psychiatrist called after him: "What is that propelling pencil doing in your pocket?"

"It is being a propelling pencil."

"Do those white bits, then, mean that you are a proper officer cadet?" his father asked for the third time.

"Fully fledged. And I carry an officer's stick. If I get through the course I'll be Second Lieutenant Graveson in three months' time."

"Well, Dan, I'm proud of you. You've done something at last. That uniform. Doesn't he look smart, Bryan?"

Bryan, from his armchair, said: "Thank God someone in this house looks smart. He looks healthy, too. Vitamin-packed. Killing must be good for you."

"I haven't slaughtered any Japs, like you did."

"I'm sorry. I got it all wrong. It is training to be a killer that is so good for you. Instruction in annihilation stimulates the hormones. Do you suffer from spots or backache? Have you got a bad leg? Have three months' fun with a bayonet and feel young again!"

"Just because you took five years to reach Corporal—"

"That's enough!" their father said. "We're going out to dinner. To celebrate. I've booked a table. So stop quarrelling, you two, while I go up and shave."

"Doesn't he shave in the morning any more?" asked Dan, when he had gone.

"It's Saturday," said Bryan.

But he would not let go.

"Yes, we're proud of you, Dan. We'll sit at home in the next war, being blown to atomic smithereens, happy in the knowledge that you're at the front winning glory!"

"You were mighty glad of the atom bomb when it stopped the war and brought you home."

Bryan stood up.

"Glad? You bloody fool! You sodding bloody little baby!"

"I'm sorry."

39

"Perhaps I was just nearer to it than you were. But since that bomb I've felt like I had leprosy – like bits of me were dropping off."

"It brought you home," Dan insisted.

"Half dead."

Dan said: "You used to be a scientific humanist."

"Labels going cheap! Scientific what? Tell it to the Japs. They're still dying from an overdose of science. Have you heard the latest from the States? They say a cure for radiation sickness is theoretically possible. Spread the glad news in Hiroshima and Nagasaki. Scientists may even now be tackling the theoretical problem of raising the one hundred and twenty-eight thousand Japanese dead."

"It's not the scientists, it's war, and the causes of war—"

"General Graveson begins to think! Who ordered you to think?"

Their father came in, in his dressing gown, soap frothing his face. A white blob fell on the carpet.

"You'll wear your uniform, Dan?"

"Of course. I'll have to press it, though. Have you got an iron?"

Bryan said: "In the kitchen, by the bread bin. Sorry, Dad, I can't come tonight – I don't feel so good. Got the shivers. Perhaps I'll join you later for a drink."

"Please come," Dan said. "I want you to."

"Some other time. Sorry."

Dan went to press his uniform, his father to finish shaving. Bryan watched the soap bubbles sink into the carpet.

Gilt and green nudes danced among flowers round the walls. Tablecloths and waiters' shirtfronts glistened in the artificial gloom.

"It's very smart. Costs a fortune. But you don't get made an officer every day," his father said.

"I've told you so many times. I've got a three-month course to get through yet."

"You'll do it. You can get anything you really try for. I've always said you were the clever one."

"No. Bryan is."

"Why don't you two get on these days? You used to."

"He's so ratty. He blows up over nothing."

"You must give him time to settle down," his father said. "I'm worried about him. He never sees anybody or wants to do anything. He doesn't sleep, just walks about all night – we meet in the kitchen at two in the morning and eat cornflakes! If only he had some friends – especially a girlfriend. He needs one. Any man does."

"I suppose so."

Waiters handed them each a huge menu.

"Have anything you like, Dan. Have the best. Do you like smoked salmon? And there's a whole capon cooked in wine, with asparagus or mushrooms."

"I want something extraordinary and rare that I've never had before."

His father ordered oysters, lobster Newbourg, Bœuf Stroganoff. He studied the wine list.

"We'll have a good claret – Léoville Lascases '28. You'll have to learn about these things now, Dan."

There was a cabaret. A fat little man played a grand piano. He composed medleys from popular songs shouted at him by the diners. "Smoke Gets in Your Eyes", shouted his father. "That's a grand old one. Your mother's favourite."

A girl sang. The lights went low and she danced, chased by a white spotlight. Her shiny dress fell in a heap on the floor. Two chorus girls joined her, hiding her with long fluffy fans. She held a fan herself and moved around, followed by the two girls. For seconds at a time Dan could see the girl's white-lit nude body as the fans hesitated. It was intentional. He glanced at his father.

"Have a liqueur, Dan. For officers only. Green Chartreuse."

"I'm sozzled."

"There's someone I would like you to meet, Dan."

"As long as it's not Auntie Lulu. I can't stand Auntie Lulu."

"I haven't seen Lulu for a long time. We've been very alone, your brother and I."

"I know."

"It's been too much. But you could help, Dan, if you wanted to."

"Me help you? That's a new one!"

"We'll see. Let's go now."

They drove through the West End. Dan sat in front next to his father. He felt warm and sleepy. The car pulled up outside a block of flats.

"Let's have a goodnight drink, Dan. And you can meet Helen."

In the self-operated lift there were six black studs with clear silver numbers. His father pressed "3".

"Darling! What a lovely surprise!" she said.

She was thin. Red hair. Young.

"And I know who this is. Come in, Daniel. Let me take your coat. What will you have?"

"Nothing, thanks – had too much already."

"Don't be silly; have a small gin."

"I'm not silly. No thanks."

His father said: "Helen's only trying to—"

"I know that. It's very nice of you. But I just couldn't take a drop more. 'Specially as I think I'll have to drive Dad home!"

"We'll have coffee," she said. "I'll put the kettle on."

Dan sat in one deep armchair, and his father sat in another.

"It's a lovely room," Dan said.

"Yes. Dan, I've known Helen for some time. She's been wonderful to me. I know you'll get on well with her."

"Of course I will."

She poured the coffee:

"It's a wonderful machine, darling; it doesn't clog up like the French one."

"I thought the chromium sieve plate would be an improvement."

"It makes very good coffee," said Dan.

She uncrossed her legs and got up to pour Dan a second cup. She leant over him.

"My, you look swell in that uniform."

"Thank you. And that's a very nice dress."

His father smiled.

"I'll take them in," Dan said.

He collected the coffee cups, put them on the tray, carried them into the kitchen. He washed them under the tap and placed them on the stainless-steel draining board. He looked for a drying-up cloth. He went back to the room to ask Helen. They were standing up and kissing hard in the well-lit centre of the room.

"I'm sorry."

"Come and kiss Helen goodnight, Dan," his father said quite loudly.

"No."

Dan could see he was holding her hand very tightly.

His father said: "Well, we've had our goodnight kiss. So it's time to go."

Dan picked up his army greatcoat from the back of a chair. "You stay. I can easily get home by Tube. It's a direct line – no changes."

He had one arm through his coat sleeve.

"Don't be silly," his father said.

"Seems to be my silly night."

He was feeling vaguely for the other armhole.

They drove home together, with the car radio playing dance music.

He blobbed out the first big triangle. Two triangles left, eight oblongs, fifty-six circles. An infantry officer must excel the best of his men in anything he may order them to do. Assault course, route march, musketry, manoeuvres, rope-climbing, weapon training, swimming, fencing, rugger, drill. Drill. No time to think? It is intentional, you are going to be an officer, not a philosopher. Lectures on tactics, man-management, venereal diseases, regimental history, Russia, Korea, Malaysia, mess etiquette, signals, strategy, leadership. Cadets when dressed in civilian clothes will wear trilby hats. Cadets will not engage in conversation with other ranks. Dan stumbled from day to day, counting the days. On Sundays after church parade, when he walked in the town, he wore his officer-type raincoat, carried his officer's cane and once or twice was saluted by young national servicemen.

He didn't care that he was an officer.

"Congratulations! Of course you'll be coming home for your leave," his father wrote. It seemed Bryan was shamming ill again, sitting in a deckchair in the garden, staring, or lying in bed all day. The idea clearly was for Dan to sit with him, spend his leave playing chess, reading Proust aloud, making coffee, being polite to Helen, chatting, visiting relations in his new uniform. No. He was going to have a good time.

He drew his first month's officer's pay, wrote home to say that he had already arranged a holiday "with some newly commissioned officer friends". And by the way, he would not need the five pounds a month any more – thanks for sending it so regularly.

He packed a bag and, alone in a taxi, went to the railway station.

"Single to Llangollen, please."

He loved the sound of the name; that was why he had chosen it.

He booked a room at a hotel. A steamy-hot day. He walked in the park, searching. He knew he didn't care what she was like, as long as he could have her without you or anyone or her knowing.

A girl lay on the grass in front of him. Her hair spread a pool of blond on the green. Her body spread-eagled, arms and legs wide, cheek against the warm lawn. The earth curved against her tummy and thighs and breasts. He felt the weight of heat in the leaves. Minute eyes of birds winked. A slow plane murmured by. She raised herself so he could see into her blouse. Her breasts moved with her breathing: lowering to brush the ground, then rising barely to touch it. A grasshopper, conspicuous on the smooth lawn, was jumping away to shelter. He caught it gently: pale green, dark green, streaks of hazel brown. He took it to her.

"Look at this."

"He's lovely" – soft Welsh voice; "let him go now."

She pulled his fingers apart, and the insect hopped out and away.

"Did you hear about the pea-catcher?" he asked.

"Tell me."

"A man stood on a high, flat roof, threw a pea up, took a step back and caught it in his mouth, threw a pea up, took a step back and caught it in his mouth, threw a pea up, took a step back, fell a thousand feet, feet first. It's an old Welsh folk tale taught me by my Granny."

"No."

"No, I made it up."

"I can see you talk a lot."

"Too much."

His hand played with her heavy fair hair, slid inside her blouse, held her breast, squeezed till his nails bit deep, felt the nipple rise hard in his palm. He strayed, searching and feeling, beneath her wide skirt.

"Let's go over there, to the trees," she said.

They walked easy together, arms round waists, to the shadow of the trees. He stretched beside her, moved closer, lay over her, in.

"I love you," he said.

"You say that easily."

"Can you make love without loving?"

"Don't be silly – of course I love you. I saw you come into the park, wandering round, and I thought you were lovely."

"What's your name?"

"Deirdre Watkins. I work in a shop. But I'm studying fashions, to be a designer."

"I'm Lieutenant Daniel Graveson – just call me Dan."

"My brother's in the army," she said; "I thought you were something like that."

They lay close, without talking.

She said: "Have you seen our swans?"

She took him to see the lake, over the other side of the park. They watched the swans floating slowly, careful, deceiving. He was dizzy with them, felt their softwhiteness. Two swans together suddenly whizzed off the water, skinning the surface with their feet, like waterskiers. They fluttered heavily around, realized the air was not for them, came skidding down, bottoms first. Ducks bounced on the small waves.

An alien, starched Scottish nanny sat on the bench beside them, lecturing her neat child:

"It's fesh, not wishes, fesh, not wishes. It's time you were learning to say the few words you do say properly. Do you want a sweet?"

"No."

"Thank you."

"Fank you."

A moment later: "Nanny, can I have a sweet?"

"Please."

"Pease."

Across the lake, a herd of mauve-and-white school-girls giggled and yelped, like flamingos drinking the Amazon. An intermittent "peep" came from an angry schoolteacher blowing her whistle – the toneless cry of an unimaginative bird.

A brilliant scarlet speedboat went mad in the middle of the lake, whining round in small circles. A big boy in a striped blazer told them:

"It's got enough petrol to keep that up for three days."

"Hurrah!" Dan said.

"We'd better be going, Dan – there's a storm coming."

They hurried back the way they had come. They reached the trees just in time. Came a maniac intensity of the sun; the shadowed side of sunlit leaves showed black, veinless. Pearly pregnant evening light invaded the afternoon. Rain fell grey against blue-black trees. They moved to where the trees were so thick that the sunlight was always shut out: no grass, only bare earth under layers of dead leaves. They were safe and dry. They looked out. A huge weight of rain drove like iron across the park, soaking, drenching, flooding, making the lawns wallow in water, forcing water into the flowerbeds, compelling the flowers to gulp and swallow hundredweights of water.

It drizzled. Raindrops filed along twigs. Budge up. Budge up. Drops dropped from leaf to leaf to ground. "While it's pouring it's driest under the trees, but afterwards it's wettest," she said.

It stopped. The last waters sluiced away. The air was clear.

A police car zizzed past them, microphone bellowing. Among the incomprehensible syllables Dan heard "Graveson". Impossible. The car was away and turned a corner. A grave young policeman walked on the other side of the rainshining street, impregnable in helmet, cape, waterproof boots. Dan told her about his brother's mock German:

49

"LuftwaffenBomben, Watford-Bypass gebomben, Auntie-Dolly gebomben, Ark Royal ein zwei
drie gebomben, Corporal Graveson gebomben,
Schikelgrüber über alles gebomben…"

They held hands past the hotel receptionist. In the
corridor he joked:

"Do you come here often?"

"Of course not. Do you think I'm that kind of girl?"

"At least you've heard about 'that kind of girl'. I didn't
know they had them in Llangollen."

"If you don't stop, I'm going straight home."

"Only kidding."

Arm round her waist, hand on the doorknob, he
kissed her.

On the carpet, just by the door (it had been pushed
under he door) lay a telegram.

NO.

"Your brother."

His fist was through the wardrobe; the mirror inside
was battered. He waved his fist about so that it bled
all over the fawn carpet, spattering it with purplish
stains.

The girl stood still, one hand white on the mock-
walnut dressing table, looking at the stains. She packed
his things into his bag, went downstairs to explain to
the manager.

"He was very understanding," she said.

She handed him his bag.

"I'll never see you again."

He didn't say anything.

He could not decide whether to walk to the station or get a taxi. It was not far, yet the bag was heavy. Platform one. Which platform? Platform one.

Early morning. He fumbled at the burglarproof double lock. Helen opened the door.

"Hello Dan. Glad you could come so quickly. Your father is upstairs."

The house was ordinary. The dead body had been taken to hospital to make sure it was dead. He opened the door of their room. His father was sitting up in bed, backed by pillows, reading the *Daily Mail*. Dan said nothing, because he could not think of anything to say.

Doors of expensive cars slammed heavy. Husbands waited while wives titivated. Thicker greyer overcoats from Leeds greeted slick, tight London ones. Stretched and skinny car reflections had squeezed waists, bodies split into two shrinking pears or tears. Ladies' sharp high heels spiked between the new grey gravel stones; men trod the gravel down. Stone cemetery arch, square cemetery building of stone. Foreign, clean, preserved from contact with the countryside. Chemical sprays and regular scrubbing with disinfectant killed small creepers and scraps of moss. Not a fleck of grass, not a living insect survived to spoil the stone. They filed in, past a pile of broken prayer books heaped on a backless chair. They edged round the walls, chatted hushedly, continually. No coffin – only an oblong space of floor. Outside, somewhere, the body lay in its warm, brown varnished box.

"Move in a little closer if you please, thank you," the priest said. Like a market salesman to his customers. Were they the customers, or was the thing in the box? It depended whether the funeral expenses were charged to the deceased's estate or were paid by the surviving relatives. Dearly beloved. The priest was enjoying his rich voice. Cut off in his prime. Splendid young man. Loyal son and brother. Credit to his church. Brilliant mind and wonderful promise. Mourned by all who remember his loving nature. Dust unto dust. Recitative without end. He towed them down the long path to the yellow trench to watch the coffin dumped in. The body in the sheet in the coffin in the earth was in the universe.

> "Unassuming, unpretending,
> Straight the Path of Life he trod,
> May his bliss be never ending
> Thro' the mercies of his God."

Oh God.

Chapter 4

BROTHER OFFICERS GATHERED round him.
"Fighting for freedom and democracy with the
Yanks in Korea? You can't believe that rubbish!" Dan
was saying.

"Another whisky?" Lieutenant Crabbe stooped over
the siphon; hard head, thick ginger stubble. He had a
parachute badge and medals.

"Here's a stiff one. Or would you prefer vodka?"

"Thanks. Remember Hiroshima. A hundred and
twenty-eight thousand bodies. What colossal contempt
they must feel for us with our measly machine guns."

"You mentioned that before."

"Then tell me, who profits from the war? Korea? China?
The answer may show who started it."

Someone said: "Those Yankee millionaires you were
talking about, with their arms factories—"

"Yes," said Dan, "and there were five million American
unemployed before the arms drive solved that problem

overnight. There's no unemployment or arms manufacturers in the New China."

"They produce a deal of arms."

"But not privately," Dan said.

"Does that make any difference?"

"It's a long story. And I must get to bed. I'm
drunk."

"Wait a bit," Crabbe said. "So the North Koreans are
fighting for peace and independence? Is that right?
Let's get the whole thing perfectly clear."

"That's an over-simplification... but I can't think
straight. I must owe you all buckets of whisky."

"Think nothing of it. It's been a pleasure."

Lieutenant Gerson, an attached officer from the
Education Corps, spoke for the first time:

"Let's talk about something else, for Heaven's sake."

"Hey, don't spoil the fun," Crabbe said.

Dan blinked.

"Fun?"

He walked over to the mantelpiece, stood with
his back to them. Eleven sharp tings sang from
the glasscased clock. He knew they had followed
him across the room. He watched the moving parts
inside the clock swinging and linking, teeth biting
precisely into delicate revolving cylinders. He heard
the scrape of windows being fastened. He looked
down at his reflection in the polished silver tray,
on which letters addressed to officers were laid.
He turned round. They had formed a halfcircle
close to him.

"I must get back," he said quietly; "I've some reading to do." (Lenin on Imperialist War* – not one of them had read a book like that.)

"Don't go yet – it's been so interesting listening to you. Quite an education."

He wondered where his hat was; he couldn't leave without it – had to have it for parade in the morning. He moved towards the door. A major stood in front, his tummy stuck out. Dan half saw a brown boot flick out, felt his ankle crack. He put his hands out as he fell, felt the carpet slide against his palms. A hand of iron grabbed his wrist; another twisted back his arm. Crabbe knelt down and spoke to him:

"Now look here, we don't want to break up the mess. Will you come out like a man?"

"What's happening?... Yes."

He was bundled outside in the middle of eight or nine of them. The cold foggy air hit him. They marched him along a gravel path, then onto grass.

"What good will this do? There's problems to solve, but this is not the way."

"Christ, he never stops."

He thought, "God, what are they going to do to me? I can't speak to them. No way of getting at them." He slithered his heels against the ground. They pushed and punched him along.

They were behind the cookhouse, among smelly piles of rubbish and open dustbins. They stopped and held him. Two of them levered up the cast-iron cover to the grease pit. Stink came up. They shoved him in.

He managed to hold his body above the slime; there was only the smell. Then a hand at the back of his neck pushed his face into the grease, held it there.

He was out, spluttering, yelling after them: "Fascists! Fascists!"

They'd gone. He sicked up onto the grass.

He arrived at breakfast very late next morning, after all the junior officers had gone. A major and a colonel sat at one end of the long oak dining table. He sat on his own. On his way out he picked up an envelope from the silver tray and read, on a piece of cheap lined paper: "Meet me for coffee at Lyons, 7.30 p.m. this evening. Gerson."

Lyons was crowded. Everyone seemed old or middle-aged. He could not see Gerson. He queued up, bought two cups of tea, sat next to an old grey man who was excitedly reckoning figures down the side of a newspaper. Dan poured sugar into his tea, aiming the stream to burst the bubbles round the side of his cup.

Gerson came in, sat opposite, saying:
"Glad you could make it."

Dan looked straight at the eyes – pale behind steel-rimmed spectacles – pale lips, thin fair hair. Gerson asked the waitress, an old African woman, to bring him a packet of cigarettes.

Dan said: "What do you want to see me about?"
"I want to have a talk with you."
"Hullo."
"Seriously. I want to know what you are trying to do."
"What do you mean?"

Dan was annoyed to see Gerson continually glancing round the room. A nervous habit.

"All this revolutionary talk," Gerson said. "Red Flag-wagging like a ten year old."

"I have certain principles—"

"Why not keep them to yourself?"

"It's those captains and majors. I want to kick their teeth in."

"You are in a bad way. Don't you know they're laughing at you?"

"I don't care."

"Yes you do – you're not so stupid. I don't know what your job is or what you're trying to do. Frankly, I don't trust you enough to tell you anything MI5 don't already know. I've been fifteen years in the party – too long to take chances. But if you care about peace, and want to do something effective—"

"What could we do?" Dan asked.

"Make a demonstration, a gesture. Have you ever gone chalking?"

"Slogans on walls? No. But that's brilliant! Let's cover the camp with hammers and sickles."

The old man on Dan's left looked up, interested.

Gerson smiled: "Lucky we live in England. Tell me, what is the main political task here today?"

"Peace…"

"Right. The reaction to hammers and sickles would be 'Help! Russian spies!' Would that tend towards peace or war?"

"The symbol of workers and peasants—"

Gerson interrupted: "Have you seen many peasants lately?"

"Thousands."

"Being peasantless," said Gerson, "is a British peculiarity of great political significance. But that's another matter."

"Then what shall we do? Let's decide now."

"No, I must go. Think about it. But for Christ's sake keep your mouth shut. If you must talk, talk to the men – that way you may learn something. Go down to their lines, or to the public bars – even the education centre. Get to know them. You'll find one or two good ones."

Dan sat looking at Gerson's teacup. A pale-brown skin had formed on the untouched tea. The waitress asked: "You want this, sir?"

"No – thank you very much indeed."

He put the cup with the cups, and the saucer on the pile of saucers on her tray. He looked at her tea-stained overall, the blue cotton skirt with yellow flowers peeping beneath it, thin liquorice legs. How could those skinny ankles bear her weight, hold up that huge bottom? How steeply under her skirt those legs must swell out into giant thighs! She should be sitting in a rocking chair surrounded by grandchildren. Gerson had not said "thank you" for the cigarettes.

Standing in the officers' latrine a week later, they decided to paint on the ammunition store: JOIN THE MOVEMENT FOR PEACE. It was, in Gerson's phrase, "the correct slogan". Dan thought it was too long.

Gerson said: "It can't be helped. Those words are essential. There may be another comrade along to help us."

"Another comrade"! Dan felt he had been knighted.

Hidden by a rolling, heavy midnight fog, Dan waited just outside the camp. He felt safe in the fog and darkness. Gerson loomed up, nosing around, looking for him. Dan kipped round behind him, pushed a stick in his back and roared:

"Welcome, Comrade!"

"For Christ's sake, have some sense," Gerson snapped.

"Can't you take a joke?"

"Yes. Where's the brush?"

"You were bringing it."

"Hell. Now what can we do? We can't paint with our bare hands."

"I'll find something," Dan said.

He ran off and returned twenty minutes later, bearing, like an Olympic flame, his shaving brush.

"The best I could find. All the paintbrush shops are shut. It's a capitalist conspiracy."

"Watch out for sentries," Gerson said; "you know what happens if we're caught."

They crept across the battalion football field, then through lines of elephantoid field guns.

"Down!"

Dan flopped on the squelchy earth. Ten yards ahead, a sentry stood, heavy like a lead soldier, staring. His slung rifle poked awkwardly out of his khaki cape. Gerson, crawling correctly as he had been taught in basic training, moved away, quick and quiet. Dan crawled after, feeling ridiculous.

They reached the ammunition store. Gerson unwrapped a paint tin.

"Take it," he said. "You paint first, and I'll keep watch. A short whistle means danger."

He folded and pocketed the brown paper.

"It's oil paint, I'm afraid, which is tricky, because it stains your clothes. Be careful."

The hut was built of corrugated-iron sheets. It had once been painted light green. In places the paint had come away, showing rusty orange beneath; elsewhere it bubbled up in wide blisters or formed a separate corrugated skin of thin green. Dan scrubbed the paint on. Green specks and slivers mixed with dollops of white showered over him. The letters began huge and got smaller and smaller as he tired. He did the final "E" and went back to Gerson. But Gerson had gone. He returned to the wall, and with the last of the paint added an exclamation mark. The hairs of the brush were rubbed away; only the small bone handle remained.

Huts and guns and piles of junk, grey animals, jumped from the fog, lurched at him. He found he was swinging the paint tin; Gerson had not said how to get rid of it. He passed an empty oil drum which had been stood straight and painted shiny black for a general's inspection. He lifted the edge and pushed the tin inside.

In his room Dan tried to get the oil paint off his hands and uniform. He used paraffin from a lamp kept "for emergencies".

As soon as he woke he longed to go and see the slogan, but Gerson had forbidden it. He waited by the NAAFI, hoping to overhear excited conversation; he was disappointed. However, on the regimental notice board a paper had been pasted over the "afternoon programme". It read:

Important. All ranks will attend parade, regimental parade ground. 1430 hours.

A. DIGBY-SMITH. ADJUTANT.

Dan thought of going sick, or deserting. He could not find Gerson.

He marched at the head of his platoon, hearing the crunch of their boots on the concrete. His battalion formed up. The high bawl of the Sergeant Major: "Talyar-r-r-n, Talyarr-r-r-n, shun!"

The Adjutant walked slowly up and down the ranks. Dan held his breath, stared straight ahead. The Adjutant came right up to him, stood glaring, inches away. "Stand easy, Graveson. Now, let's have a look at your chaps."

Dan relaxed.

"Just a security check," the Adjutant murmured. "Now men," he turned to them, "each section in turn will come smartly to attention and all ranks will hold their hands smartly in front of them."

As each man begged for alms, the Adjutant walked gravely by, accompanied by Lt. Graveson. With the tips of his fingers he turned over each pair of hands, and looked at them keenly. A man with big grimy hands and dirty bitten nails said:

"I work down the boilers, sir."

"Hold your tongue, man! Don't you know you're on parade? Speak when you're spoken to!"

The Adjutant looked up at the man, who was a foot taller, and snapped:

"A disgraceful turnout. No excuse. Take that man's name, Mr Graveson."

He smiled at the Sergeant and glanced at his hands too. "Carry on, Mr Graveson!"

"Yessir! Platoo-oo-oon, by the right, qu-i-i-i-ck march!"

Since 1747 Friday had been regimental mess night. From seven o'clock until nine, all junior officers stood about the mess lounge in dress uniform, drinking, chatting, waiting for the CO to lead the regiment into dinner. Dan stood fingering the stem of his glass. He heard Gerson's clear, clipped voice:

"…Hunt ball on Tuesday."

"Where the devil is one to procure scarlet tails these days?" Crabbe asked.

Dan stood near them.

"That's a problem for you regulars," said Gerson; "I think I'll trot along in my DJ."*

A pause. They sipped whisky.

"So you're a national serviceman," Crabbe said. "What were you in before?"

"I'm a lawyer," Gerson replied.

"Defending swindlers and murderers, eh?"

"Not exactly. I dealt mainly with land law and property."
"Oh yes."

Crabbe finished his drink.

"What'll you have?" Crabbe asked Gerson.

Dan stood quiet.

"And you, old chap?" Crabbe turned to him.

"No thanks," Dan said.

Crabbe brought back two whiskies. On the way he had been thinking.

"What is land law exactly? Sounds a bore."

"Strangely enough, land law is ninety per cent of the law, although less than a tenth of the people own land."

"Why is that?" Dan asked innocently.

"Because most of our laws were made by nineteenth-century landed gentry, whose first concern was with their own property."

Crabbe left them. Dan said to Gerson:

"Next week he'll be telling the mess that land law is ninety per cent of the law and what are they going to do about it!"

"Really?" Gerson said. "Please excuse me a moment."

Dan rolled the stem of his glass between his fingers. The chat rose and fell around him. He lit a cigarette.

At a quarter to nine something unusual happened. The Adjutant stood at one end of the lounge banging the table with his glass, calling:

"Quiet, gentlemen. One moment please, gentlemen. Quiet."

There was some whispering. The Adj. had drunk only two gins the whole evening – a sign something was brewing.

"I do apologize, gentlemen. But the security chaps have a thing on their mind. And you know what that means. We'll just have to play along with them. This afternoon we had a special parade and inspection for all non-commissioned ranks. Now Intelligence is so damned thorough – suppose we should thank Heavens for it – it seems it will be necessary for us in the mess to undergo a similar check. A mere formality for completeness, you understand, gentlemen. All junior officers then, if you please, gentlemen, form along that wall, and we can finish in five minutes."

A roar of voices all talking at once – some protesting, some making jokes, all asking what it was all about. Rapidly the Adjutant walked past, glancing at their hands held out. He made it clear that it was not his idea, but that he was formally carrying out superior orders. Dan remembered the early morning spent scrubbing his hands almost raw with pumice stone and scalding water. By electric light the streaks of white across his hands barely showed. The Adjutant checked and passed him without a sign. Perhaps he lingered a moment. Dan could not be sure.

A week had passed. The slogan had been blacked over by military police before more than a dozen men had seen it. No one had quite understood it; there had been some puzzled talk – a paragraph in the *Movement for Peace Newsletter* under "News from the Branches".

"How's it going, old boy?"

The Adjutant's hand rested on Dan's shoulder. This treatment was reserved for field officers and RSMs.*

"Quite well, thank you, sir."

"Could you take ten minutes off this afternoon? The CO would like a word with you."

"Yes sir. What time would be convenient, sir?"

"What about 1430 hours?"

"Well, I'm down for firing practice then, sir."

The Adjutant frowned.

"Never mind about that, Graveson."

"Very well, sir."

Rarely did the Commanding Officer talk officially with a person of inferior rank without being supported by his menials: Second in Command, Adjutant, Regimental Sergeant Major, Aide-de-Camp. Dan was relieved, therefore, to find Colonel York quite alone.

"Glad to see you, Graveson."

The Colonel did not get up from his heavy leather chair. He sat like an old lion, with whiskery brows, paws for hands and a way of turning his head round slowly.

"Do sit down. Smoke?"

"No, thank you, sir."

"Wise man."

Dan sat straight on his wooden chair, his hands on his lap. The Colonel glanced down at a file of papers and a copy of Queens Regulations. He pulled at the lobe of his ear, flicked the bristles of his moustache. Dan had seen him behave like this when talking with very senior officers.

"It's about this security report, Graveson. It seems that, on the afternoon, 3rd July – that is, Monday last – during the delivery of a lecture to P Company, you were guilty of conduct which amounted to incitement to mutiny. What have you to say?"

"I have absolutely no idea what it is all about, sir. There must be some mistake."

"I don't think so," the Colonel murmured. "You were giving instruction on the twenty-five-pounders?"*

"That is possible."

"You initiated a discussion on the value of the weapon?"

"I prefaced my lecture with a general description of the gun, including its cash cost. I had obtained the information from the regimental office."

"Indeed. What followed?"

"I'm not sure, sir."

"Come, come, Graveson. I have the details here. But I prefer to know your side of the picture. '*Audi alteram partem*',* you know."

"Well sir, the figures in thousands of pounds meant nothing to the men. So I may have translated them into terms they could understand. One gun equals twenty motor cars, for example."

"Or so many council houses or hospital beds? Did you even find it necessary to discuss the position of old-age pensioners?"

"No sir, that was one of the men."

"Did you not ask the men to 'vote' on which they would 'prefer to have their money spent on'?"

"It was not quite like that, sir."

"You understand, Graveson, that I cannot have one of my officers carrying on like this."

"Sir."

"No one sympathizes with the pensioners more than I do, but this kind of talk, in the regiment's time – it's sheer pacifism. Or worse. You join the army to do a job. A job for your country. If you would prefer to be on the other side – very well, then. But you cannot have it both ways!"

"It seems to me—"

"Don't argue with me. And don't interrupt. The fact is, Graveson, I am instructed to request you to resign your commission with effect from the first of next month. You will have twelve days' leave until that date."

"It's a terrible shock, sir."

"I'm sorry, Graveson. I've never had a thing like this in my regiment. I cannot concern myself with personal feelings. It's more than a question of regimental discipline – the matter is out of my hands."

"I must have time to think about it."

"That is impossible. I formally request you to resign."

Dan stood up.

"I cannot do that, sir. I consider I have the right of any citizen to hold political views and express them, so long as I do not break army or civil law. If I am charged with an offence, then I wish to be tried by court martial. The publicity will no doubt create—"

"You may take whatever action you think fit," the Colonel said decisively. "But I must warn you that a number of other matters, including a recent occurrence you no doubt have in mind, would certainly be raised against you in the event of your acting foolishly. A court martial, needless to say, has the power to award the heaviest penalties. I still hope we may settle this matter man to man without unpleasantness."

"I am only asking for my democratic—"

"Yes, yes, yes. Very well; that will be all, Graveson. I advise you to consider your position carefully."

"I will, sir. Thank you, sir."

In the outer office, the Adjutant handed him a typed document:

"…commanded by Her Majesty to inform you that, following certain admissions, the army council have decided that Lieutenant Daniel Graveson should be called upon to… resign his commission… Should he neglect or refuse to submit his application to resign within fourteen days… steps will be taken with a view to terminating the said commission with effect from…"

"Will you sign for it, sir?" the clerk said.

"What?"

"To show you received it, sir."

"No."

The clerk looked towards the Adjutant, who said: "Never mind about that now."

He marched smartly across the parade ground among the drilling squads and companies. Orders of command whined and roared over his head. He tried to appear as if he had important business to attend to. But he did not know where to go. A sergeant glanced at him sideways – did he know? How long would the news take to travel round the camp?

He found himself at the education centre. Forlorn and empty. Dusty posters told stories in pictures about first aid, fire drill, artificial respiration. Men with moustaches demonstrated life-saving. Old coloured maps showed the distribution of barley, wheat and sugar beet in the neighbouring fields. Who cared? A film of dust covered the globe's northern hemisphere. The centre was mainly used as a source of drawing pins. The bottom pins from all the posters had been borrowed, leaving pinholes and blobs of rust in the flapping corners. Old Major Caulfield came in:

"What can I do for you, Graveson?"

"I'm waiting for Mr Gerson, if that's all right, sir."

"By all means."

Dan watched the sagging face, the huge dark veins in the hands.

"Did I ever show you these, Graveson?"

Glossy photographs of a chubby bouncing man.

"I was army breast-stroke champion in those days – nineteen thirty-two."

He still wore his Army Swimming Club blazer and tie. Gerson came in. A spot in the palm of the Major's hand was then travelling towards his heart – a thickening, a slight thickening of the blood, easing towards the muscular heart to cover over and close two hefty pounding vital bloodfilled arteries and stop the flow of blood. He'd be gone and turned to slime.

"The granting of a commission," said Gerson, "is part of the Queen's prerogative. There need be no court martial, no appeal. That which Her Majesty giveth, she may also take away. But you can make a political fight. Do you want to?"

"I'll do anything."

"Don't underrate the strength of the forces against you. Don't start a battle you can't win. Will your own platoon speak up for you? Can you depend on any of the NCOs,* or your brother officers? What about your family?"

"I don't expect much help from anyone else."

"I see. Well, how do you propose to start the campaign?"

"I am prepared to follow out any plan the Communist Party proposes."

Gerson said nothing for a minute, then:

"In my opinion, you should resign with as little fuss as possible."

* * *

"Dan! We're going to Helen's. Put your uniform on," his father called up the stairs.

"I'm sick to death of the bloody uniform."

"Do as you please."

Then, on the last day of his leave, a letter arrived, addressed to "265546221 Pte.* Graveson, D". His father held it out to him:

"What's all that about?"

Dan read the short printed letter.

"Good news. I've been posted to another unit. It's quite close by – Epping Forest. On the Central Line. I'll be able to get home for the weekends."

"Aren't you an officer any more?"

"The envelope? That's just a typist's error."

In the car, outside the Tube station, his father said: "You're in some trouble."

"It's nothing."

"Then why the long face? I'm a bit older than you—"

"Old enough to be my father."

"—and I still know a thing or two. If only you'll tell me what kind of a jam you're in—"

"Raspberry. I've been demoted, temporarily."

"I knew it. What happened?"

"Well, the CO is an absolute tyrant. Real guards disciplinarian. Punishment parades for the slightest mistake. He's completely inhuman. I led a deputation of the men to complain, I threatened we'd see our MPs and get publicity in the papers... it was nearly a mutiny."

"What about your communist friend – whatsisname – Gherkin?"

"He thinks I did a good job."

"But he's leading the troops from behind?"

"No. In the developing political situation—"

"I don't give two pins for the blasted situation. He got you into this mess – can he get you out?"

"The Government is tottering—"

"And a puff of your adolescent emotion is going to bring the Government down! You've been cashiered and ruined your career and you still shout *Daily Worker* slogans at me."

"You're doing the shouting, Dad."

"You'll miss your train. Better go now. I was going to tell you: I've been trying to get you into the Inns of Court, to read for the Bar. I only hope they don't ask me for your army record."

They went into the station. His father bought the ticket, handed it to him with a five-pound note.

"You'll be needing this now, Dan."

"Thanks."

"Don't thank me – keep out of trouble. And you'll find a law book in your bag. No harm in a bit of swotting, if you get the chance."

"I will. Thanks for everything. Give my love to Helen. Cheerio, Dad."

"Goodbye."

Alone in the carriage, he dumped his bag beside him. He put his feet up and glared horribly out of the window. A bald old man, unperturbed, got in and went to sit where the bag was. Dan swung the bag up to put it on the rack. Plunk! He hit and smashed a light bulb and bits of glass pattered over the miserable blue suit.

The girl opposite crossed her long legs, lifted one leg to fiddle with the heel of her high-heeled shoe. Past the band at the top of her stocking (reinforced to give the suspender something to hook into) that inner surface of her thigh was her softest and sweetest part. In a tunnel the train stopped dead. The one bulb gave a bead of light.

"Aren't you frightened?"

She didn't answer. He stretched to get something from his bag. As he did so his army boot struck her leg hard. When the train brought them out of the tunnel he saw the heavy dark mark on her leg caused either by a bruise on the skin showing through the stocking or by the black polish from his boot. As she got out at the next station, she said to him, in a strong cockney voice: "If you're the kind of miserable little sod who takes it out on young girls, the sooner you're locked up the better."

The train swung out towards the strange fresh air, rising from a concrete ditch topped by level railings, passing another train sliding in the opposite direction into the long hole: first the head, then the long body, last the tail light spinning away and down. He looked into the back windows of grey slum houses, grey lace curtains, bits of kitchen, geysers and cupboards. Further from London life got easier. Hundreds of oblong back gardens, trees, television aerials, multicoloured clothes on clotheslines, shirts, upside-down trousers held by pegs, one to each ankle. Outside stations in desirable residential areas massed cars waited: some for wives with spare keys, to do the shopping; others till evening to save their masters ten-minute healthy walks. Came odd hopeless triangles of desert: long grass, planks, patches of stinging nettles, pram bits, small hills of gravel; nobody owned them.

A monster black-and-yellow army sign shattered the countryside. He obeyed the arrow, walked across open heath, among beach trees and blackberry bushes. The berries were hard and green or having been picked with a morose scrap of hay left behind. The kids must be on to them as soon as the green gets tinged with pink. They are forced to eat them hard and sour, because if one leaves them as uneatable, others will risk the tummy ache. He dreaded arriving at the camp, pictured it again and again. He remembered the radio blare and the cursing, the purposeless parades, being ordered about by unintelligent sergeants.

His job was to push trolleys or carry shelves of supplies from the food store to the kitchens. He put both hands under the heavy wood shelves, which were piled with loaves, slabs of lard, bacon, bowls of potatoes. His neck muscles and the backs of his knees ached. The trolleys, mysteriously, were always empty, so they were light and easy to push. He liked pushing trolleys best. It was the most useful work he had done since joining the army.

Chapter 5

H E WAS DOWNSTAIRS EARLY, before them. The maid, on her knees in the lounge, was laying the fire; her bare legs stuck out from under her skirt. Among the plates on the breakfast table there were, as usual, two butter dishes. One, between his father's place and Helen's, held yellow heavy butter. In the other, convenient to his own place, he recognized the white flakiness of margarine. He changed the dishes over. At breakfast he spread the butter thickly, asked for more toast, kept the dish close to him. He smiled at Helen.

His father was calling for him to come out to the car immediately; he couldn't wait all morning; he, at least, had some work to do. Dan went quickly to the maid's room, stood holding the door open. She sat on the cheap bed, darning her skirt.

"Could you spare just ten bob, Joan?"

"You know I'm not paid till Friday."

"Sorry."

"Wait – I think I have two shillings."

She opened the wardrobe with a little key that had sur-vived three owners and two second-hand shops. While she searched in her handbag, he looked, ashamed, at the bits of worn carpet which didn't match. A porcelain Christ hung from a nail on the wall. Catholic pamphlets and women's magazines were piled up, tattered from being read religiously. She gave him half-a-crown.

"I'll pay you back. It's damn nice of you."

"It's nothing of the kind."

He walked from his father's office to the public library. Intently, he indexed things: a charwoman washing the tiles in the doorway of a chemist's shop; her broken shoe; a cubic yard of white hot coke in a machine thuga-thugathugathuga making asphalt; a chap looking up at a lorryful of fruit.

At a table in the reference library and reading room he struggled to study, learnt rare words, wrote sexy stories. A tired woman dragged a child to *The Nursing World* in a rack on the wall, hisswhispering:

"Michael, I'm not hurting you. Now stop it. I've got you, so your hand can't slip."

Situation vacant. *The Law of Master and Servant.* Preface. The author could not forbear to mention the generous assistance afforded him by... A ragged tanned man asked at the counter for the *Bankers' Almanac*, please. The librarian, a thin girl with tight curls permanently waved, consulted reference books about reference books.

He said: "It's all right – I'll find it."

She hurried, touched his elbow.

"It's BA 332.8."

She pointed to the shelves.

"I can get it," he said.

He hovered in the middle of the room. Reaching up on tiptoe, she put her hand on a large blue book, tips of her fingers at the top of it, her palm resting along the spine. He looked down at her shoes.

"Thanks; I'll get it," he said.

She eased the book out so that a triangle of it was away from the shelf. She walked back to the counter, past him. He stood before the books, reading their heavy-lettered titles. Hummed a bit. His long brown forefinger touched *Bankers,* did not move the book. He took his hand away. He scratched his neck inside his collar. Chapter One: Nineteenth century. Conditions of employment. The early Workmen's Compensation Acts. Whereas. A girl shook the table as she scribbled hard notes from the *Encyclopaedia Britannica.* Rubber products. She leant across the book, resting her bosom on it. As she wrote, the end of her pen, which was soured and scratched where she had nervously sucked and bitten it, jabbed into her rhythmically. He bent down to tie his laces, looked up at her beneath the table. Shadows. KOJE yelled from a newspaper headline. And the prisoners at the gateway sang their international song. "One miner's worth ten lawyers," he had said to Gerson. "Yes," Gerson had replied, "down a mine." He moved to another table and worked. As he left, at twelve, for lunch, an old lady was explaining to the chief librarian: "It was an anthology by Herrington – I have it so firmly in my mind. And so have you, haven't you?"

"I wouldn't say that, madam."

"You'd remembered you'd seen it."

"Well, I might have seen it on a list."

"Yes, that's right – on a list."

* * *

"Helen tells me you've been borrowing money from the maid again."

His father was tired.

"I'll pay her back."

"That's not the point. It's not nice. And I've given you twenty-five pounds this month. That means you're spending over six pounds a week. Families live on less, and you've got to."

"I don't know where it all goes. If you exploited the workers less intensively I might qualify for a government grant, and then I'd be on my own."

"Is that what you want?"

"Maybe it's what many people want."

"You're quite wrong, Dan; only the other day Helen was saying—"

"I know: 'how much she liked me'."

Dan heard the kitchen door slam. He said quickly: "Saw a loony boy this afternoon."

"Mmm."

"He was making a pig in the sky with string."

Helen jerked the door open. "Perfect timing," he thought. She saw him smile.

"What was that?" she asked.

His father said quickly: "Only a boy Dan met."

"Didn't he say 'pig' or something?"

"Yes? There's a marvellous programme on tonight. Danny Kaye."*

"He's brilliant," Dan said.

"I wonder if he passed his law exams first time," Helen said.

"Well, I'm certainly going to, if that's on your mind."

"Of course you are," said his father. "There's time for a cocktail before dinner. Dan, get the ice. Have we a fresh lemon and a little grated nutmeg, Helen?"

* * *

He sat for his exam. It would be a month until the results were published in *The Times*. He had to do something. Anything. He walked into the town hall. "I'm forming a branch of the Peace with China Committee," he announced.

"Oh, well—" said the young clerk.

"I'm told you could give me a list of local organizations."

"I'll see."

He called through a door: "Young gent here from the China people wants the orgs file."

Mumbles. Squeaks. A cardboard folder.

"'Fraid you can't take it away, but you can copy the addresses."

79

For ten days he knocked on doors, asked beekeepers, octogenarians, pacifists, Conservatives, folkdancers, scouts, Labour and Communist Party members, rose growers, trainspotters, curates, trade unionists, stamp collectors, youth leaders to stop MacArthur,* prevent international conflagration and keep their hands off China.

Sixty enthusiasts were invited to the inaugural meeting at Dan's home, Thursday evening, 7 p.m. sharp. Helen and his father went early to the cinema. Joan was told she could go after she had prepared the egg sandwiches. Bottles of light ale, which his father had ordered from the off-licence, stood in rows on the floor, and on trays tall glasses waited in twelve columns of five. Dan brought down the old Left Book Club books and strewed them around.

At seven, Rickie came, from the big house next door. He was middle-aged, a vegetarian, ran a cycling club for boys; he wore shorts. By seven thirty, two nice old ladies from the Peace Pledge Union were sitting in armchairs talking with Bert – a cross-eyed chap in a blue suit with a rucksack. At eight o'clock Bert said they needed a chairman – and would Dan open the meeting? Dan stood by the fireplace, said, Yes, well, they all knew why they had been asked, and if they agreed with the aims of the committee, they could form a branch and try to do something about it, because it was a mistake to think that the people were powerless. That was playing into the hands of the reactionaries. The people flew the bombers and fired the guns, and the people could make war impossible. They ate sandwiches, and Bert drank a quart of beer. They agreed to hold a public meeting in the church hall. Bert had some pamphlets about Peoples' China, and they all bought one. They decided to meet monthly at Bert's home. Dan was elected secretary by four votes to none.

Helen complained about the mess. His father said cigarette ash was good for the carpet, it made it grow, and he told everyone that Dan was secretary of the Peace Movement.

Dan was still in bed on Saturday morning when Helen brought up the papers.

"I can't find your name in *The Times,*" she said.

"Then I've failed."

"You're very calm about it."

"There's no point in getting hysterical," Dan said.

"What will your father say? You might show some feeling for him, after all he's done for you."

"He's a very generous man. Don't you find that?"

"You're his biggest disappointment—"

"Mind your own business."

"Your father's happiness is my business."

"Quite a profitable one."

"Take that back! Take that back!"

She was crying. He heard her sobbing and shouting in his father's room. He thought, Good – he's got something else to think about, apart from my bloody exams.

His father came in, sat on the bed.

"Do you want to give up law?" he asked.

"Of course not."

"There's no 'of course' about it. You could have passed that exam. You're not a fool. You just didn't work."

"Other chaps fail."

"You're not like them. You can do it, Dan. I only wish I had your chances – I'd be working day and night. I'll help you all I can, but you've got to do the work."

"I could study better in a place of my own. Nearer the college, to save travelling."

"All right. I'll find you a room – not too far away, so you can come home for the weekends."

The three of them had become expert at mealtime chat, but lunch was like an escalator suddenly stopped – everyone having to climb the unaccustomed stairs. Dan sat quiet, looked at his face upside down in a spoon. Helen chatted in little swoops. Up she went, then, hearing the brittle brightness, stopped awkwardly. His father knew the weight was on him, and cautiously avoided forbidden places. He pointed with his knife at the electric clock:

"That was a bad buy, Helen; it's never been right since we bought it."

Helen said: "And the trouble is you never know whether it's going to gain or lose, but our bedroom one is—"

Dan interrupted her: "It's caused by minute variations in the electric current, you know. But that steady sweep of the big hand – it's so impressive. Gets people every time."

He wondered whether they would leave his chair by the table or put it against the wall. The table was going to be very big for the two of them. Joan brought in three cups of coffee on a green plastic tray. His father glanced from her breasts to the coffee cups and back again.

Dan went to Bert's house, to see about the committee. "I'm sorry, dear, Bert's not back from work yet," his wife said. "I know he'd like to see you – he's told me about you; come in and wait – I'll make a cup of tea."

She was pregnant – about seven months gone. She shut the front door behind him: "clack" of a council house, not "clonk" like the door of his home. The house seemed as full of kids as she was: four of them – "the eldest is nine" – ran around the kitchen, into the garden and back again, up and down the stairs, got legs caught in the banisters, swiped each other with sticks, knocked over milk bottles, pushed a rusty old pram round and round the garden, climbed into the dustbin, got bits of grit in their eyes, used the dustbin lid as a shield while the others threw stones, pulled each other's hair, burst into tears, yelled, laughed, wiped dripping noses with greasy hands, sat in a puddle eating dirt, asked questions, painted on the wall "it's our wall", stood staring at flies, poked a tortoise with a stick, held it up by its shell, screaming:

"Don't drop Mr Wooby! Don't drop Mr Wooby!"

"They dropped him once and cracked him," she said.

She walked round all the time, following them, telling them off, listening to Dan, talking to him. The kettle went on whistling. Her belly pushed at him. She had a wheelbarrowful of childbelly; she wheeled it in front of her. He sat harmless on a kitchen chair, waiting for her navel to shove into his face. Her belly was covered by a skirt wrapped round it – huge pink and white blobs and big white buttons. The last three buttons hung down by their cotton threads, pulled by the kids scrambling beneath her. Like a huge mother sow she didn't crush one of them. She bent down, showing her pink underslip, and wiped or swiped bits of fluff and hair from the kids' sticky mouths, and yellowish snot from their noses.

Bert came in.

"Glad to see you here, Dan."

Hefty handclench. He poured himself a cup of tea. Through the cabbagey smell of the kitchen his sweaty smell came over. His wife lifted a baby from a pram in the corner:

"It's time for his bath."

And she pushed herself upstairs.

"Been digging trenches in the park," Bert said. "Foundations for a new school. They must have heard about my lot."

"I'm terribly sorry, Bert, I've got to give up the Peace Committee." Dan knew he was talking in a special way, slurring words and dropping aitches.

"That's all right, mate. Didn't your mum approve?"

"It's not that. I'm getting a flat in town, on my own."

"Well well," Bert said.

Chapter 6

UNSHAVED AND UNWASHED because a spider stayed circling, shrivelling, still crawling round the washbasin, he lay on the hard bed, looking at the nude on the wall, the blackblistered cold fireplace, the gas ring squatting on the lino. He sat up. Some bright bits on the carpet were spots of daylight from the other side of the earth. Tunnels made by needles. He remembered when Grandma swallowed a needle and a year later it came out of her heel. Faces, camels, goblins, birds lived in the patterned curtains; behind the window, but almost flush with it, a darkbrick neighbour wall shut out the night.

He trod down the quiet, creaking stairs, got outside. Street lights shone yellow madly at nobody. Sky men in purple overcoats and floppy pink hats played moon-football. His nose was cold. Fresh on his face light rain fell. He pounded over the ringing pavement. "Be twenty. Poise dizzy at an angle on a waterfall edge. Look down, see the white gas there. Plunge, splutter, shoot away and race away downriver." Rain fell, bounced, danced, on his pavement, which he'd put there on purpose.

He looked in at a workmen's café. He wasn't a workman. Water trickled down the misted window; it was warm inside and cold out.

Home, he flopped on the bed. Spider's a long time dying. Up once more, he put the bacon he'd bought into the saucepan he'd bought, watched the warmed fat become lucent, ooze, begin to crackle. He sniffed.

Downstairs again, to the lavatory, taking things with him. The slightly slimy stone rim refused his body warmth. He stretched his leg forwards, pressed his foot against the door to keep it shut. He read the brown-paper-covered book he had taken from his father's wardrobe. First acne, underwear, the Orient, spiritual awareness, conducive foods: cloves and saffron, black molasses. Then at last, love play, coital positions, perfect courtship, ideal marriage, advanced coital positions, notes for the obese. The other book, twisting nudes, lay on the floor. He tried to read the two together. O manufacturers of frosted glass for the windows of suburban lavatories!

The gas ring still flared in the dark room. The bacon was charred dust on the ceiling and out of the window, the floor wet with liquid saucepan. He offered himself a saucepan sandwich.

* * *

Helen's precise hand: two neat strokes sliced through the old address, and small, clear letters announced the new. The envelope contained an invitation to a party from Montague.

Frantic in the frantic centre of the frantically crammed room, Montague stood with his hairy hands in his hairy jacket pockets. Dan walked right up to and on top of him talking immediately loudly continuously. *Quel savoir-faire.* He wore his pipe, and Montague told him how well it suited him – made him look much older. Dan joined the homosexual cowboys chatting cleverly at bubbly girls. What do you do? Me Yugoslav partisan – part-time. What's your favourite colour eyes? The great eyes of camels and the eyes of men in Sainsbury's. He stopped. He'd climbed over himself. Embarrassed girls looked at each other's feet, drifted away. But she circled, dancing, a glance for him each time round. Her northern hemispheres bounced, wobbled, jumped. She looked, double-chinned, down at them, a basketful of puppies. He took her drunk, damp hand, led her into the room reserved for sexual intercourse. It was going to be lovely.

He said: "Bell fling float kite cap kiss shell hill plough panther antler elegant bending rainbow rain garden grave—"

"What are you talking about?"

"Just a game."

"Kid's game," she said; "one word leads to another. One two three. We all know that."

His head lay on her lap; he spoke to her tummy.

"Words don't describe, they point; and poets hit the source in history, the shadow behind each word. Don't slip so quick from step to step. Rest. Words are abstract isolate ancient huge, flipping and floating in coloured balloons in fanlight air. Yelp. Out it flasht. Flashtitout. Timmy begoodboynow. Guttergone. Autumn eats trees with amazing flames, leaving the indigestible bones for deadwinter."

She stared across at the bodies fiddling and squeezing and heaving.

"Why go on?" she said.

"For the prize – to dirtily prise your knees and thighs, to deliberately split your delicious infinitive."

"Oh. Well, you can get off me."

In the main room people sank by stages to the floor, spilling drinks over each other.

"Somebody stole yo' gal?" Montague asked.

"Seizing abandoned property is no larceny," Dan said.

"So you're going to be Lord Chief Justice, after all?"

"Never. My heart's not in it. I don't care who owns things."

"Your father—"

"Forget him. One death was tragic, but two made him ridiculous. Now the weight's on me, and brother, he's in for a disappointment."

"Does he ever talk about Bryan?" Montague asked.

"The dirty words in our home are 'dead wife' and 'dead son'. Never mentioned. Not a picture, not a word."

"Because the alternative to silence is a scream?"

"Because Helen's a doll, a real doll, and she mustn't be made miserable."

"If it weren't for her," Montague said, "if you were left alone with him, you'd soon find him hanging by his braces. Your father is living with Helen, and he's alive with her. But you want to camp in galleries of tinted photographs. Why dwell on death?"

"Why not wallow in it? Hell, how Grandma would have wallowed and wailed and bellowed and punched herself blue! With us each emotion is clipped like a privet hedge or a slick moustache. Throw away your lines, be polite, and after two gins be charming. That's all. But I want to learn Latin, be in the desert, kill with an axe, cover my ear in gravy, piss on their carpet, fill that bloody television set with old cod. Ours is not an icon – it's got doors, it's a triptych. Them, their actual heads and legs I love all right. But they've been suffocated by junk. They can't even cry for the dead."

He belched.

His friend stood up: "You'd better go home."

"It's too early," Dan pleaded; "let's go to the pictures, or—"

"I'm taking you to the nearest Underground."

Alone and singing in a huge lift going down. No, there was a man with him, working the lift, listening, chewing. Two big eye teeth and a thin loose lip, which he chewed. He prodded a bellysoft thumbshape into shadow. A strong spring flung the steel gate across and slammed Dan's ear out.

"Eye-Teeth!" Dan bawled, "You've knocked my bloody ear out! You and the senior lift operator and the assistant stationmaster and the stationmaster and the designer of lifts and the constructor of lifts and the minister and Her Majesty and Hieronymus Bosch and the Bishop of Bath and Wells. And I'm gonna boot the lot."

Carefully he balanced on one foot, gave a quick swing and kicked himself out onto the non-slip floor. Eye-Teeth picked him up, leant him against the tiled wall and told him he'd had a drop too much. Scraps of rag and paper lay in the lift hole, cables and weights and wheels moved steadily. Miles above, a metal voice cried: "Stand clear of the gates."

Two hundred times a day he used to yell that – yelled himself hoarse. Now he does a new recording once a year and switches on whenever he wants. Dan saw three sharp little black studs with clear silver letters: nonsec, bel, bug. He tried to hang on to the smoothtiled wettish wall.

Suddenly he was deep in people rushing on and off and anyhow. Crowds of girls, a porter with a watering can, soldiers, boys in striped scarves, actresses, dreary gentlemen. He swam along. He was going home.

* * *

They dined in the Temple, formally, on benches, enclosed by ancient coats of arms, by King Charles tiny and pointed on his thirty-foot cart horse, a gorgeous woodcarved ceiling, stained-glass windows scarlet and ultramarine, pockmarked servants, a macebearer with a mace, glossy collars and cuffs and teeth pinpointed against dark suits and the solid brown of panelled oak. Montague, Dan's guest, was impressed.

"When I went into my Dad's dress business," he said, "I never knew what I was missing. Twelve hundred a year and the night plane to Rome when the peaches are ripe is all very well, but this... this is big, Dan. It's grand, it's historical, it's feudal. The Yanks should make a colour film of it."

"You ain't seen nothin' yet," said Dan. "Here comes the procession of judges. Something to tell the grandkids."

The line of old men doddered along between the tables, near close enough to touch. The senior judge thanked the Lord beautifully for His bounteous liberality, and everyone sat down.

"Man, they're the ancientest," said Montague.

"They are indeed incredibly old, and diseased," said Dan. "And remember that I – if I sweat and strain – I may become one of those."

"It's a great incentive," said Montague. "Look at that little one – he's fantastic. Those facial muscles, that premature bulldog look. How does he do it?"

"Each morning," Dan replied, "after gargling, he informs the bathroom: 'I, Mr Justice Presley, enshrine the Constitution. I have never heard of rock and roll.' He repeats this to his wife, who says: 'Yes, dear.' He pulls on his long pants, eats a very big breakfast, is conveyed to the Courts, where, robed and throned, ten miles above the multitude, he tells working-class witnesses to 'Speak up, man!', because he can't hear a word."

"Seriously," said Montague, "what makes you so bitter?"

"Tell me why, in all history, a judge has never once said 'Put a sock in it', 'Fuck you, Jack', 'My leg itches', 'I feel awful', 'You look a lovely bit of stuff'?"

"I'll answer your question if you answer mine."

"I failed my exam."

"Again?"

* * *

"You have proved that property law is a swindle, and therefore not worth studying," his father said, "but you failed divorce too?"

"Divorce is as big a fraud as marriage. Let people do as they please. They're grown-ups. Live-together or not-live-together. Who cares?"

"The children?"

"Farm them out to mass crèches supervised by trained male nurses."

His father was counting pound notes from his wallet. "Here's ten pounds," he said. "Make it last two years."

"Did you discuss this with anyone we know?"

"Don't be stupid, Dan. Why didn't you work? If you were a bloody fool I could excuse it, but you're just drifting. Life's been too easy for you. You need a shock. If only I had my time over again... I got to London with

a five-pound note in my pocket and a wife and child in
the back of the car."

"You had a car then?"

"You know what I mean, Dan."

"Yes I do."

"You think you do. You heard about the young man
of nineteen who thought his father an idiot, and at
twenty-one he couldn't understand how—"

Dan chimed in the last words: "—the old man had
learnt so much in the last two years."

They smiled.

"I mean it, Dan. When I was your age I worked from
six in the morning till twelve at night. Sometimes
drove up to Lincoln to fetch a big load, then a quick
turn round and down to the Garden* by early morning. The other firms had drivers, but I was on my
own. We lived on sandwiches – that's what ruined
my digestion."

"I thought it was booze."

"I did things then I'd never do now. I'm old."

"You're a success. You're well off. You've built up a
business. You smoke cigars and drink whisky. You've
a beautiful redhead and a 21-inch TV. What more do
you want – ulcers?"

"I was born at the wrong time. Ten years earlier and
I'd have made a million. But those days will never come
back. There isn't the money to be made any more –
not that kind of money. I remember them coming to
me with the first idea for football pools, but I'd been
caught too often."

"So you're rich and successful and full of regrets. Why can't you understand when I say my heart's not in it?"

"Who gives a damn if your heart's not in it! My heart's not in it! Go to your beloved workers on their way to work in the morning, if you can get up that early, and ask them if their hearts are in it. You'll get some funny answers."

"Then what's the point of it all?"

"The posing of that question is a luxury you can no longer afford. You can start worrying about philosophy when you are in a steady job."

Chapter 7

H E FOUND MONTAGUE seated in his maroon upholstered swivel chair, using his two white daily sterilized telephones, consulting his stainless-steel filing cabinet, blinking at graphs, confiding in his suedette secretary, fiddling with the thermostatically controlled central-heating system. Fitness for function. Montague's function was to meet foreign buyers, note carefully that they were all unable to state precisely the quantity and quality of the goods they wished to import, and to have lunch every day with Dad and the other directors. He was able to spare Dan a few minutes, lend him four pounds and give him a note of introduction to Max Spencer, an appeals organizer for charities, who required an assistant secretary with a public-school background.

Spencer carried a yellow glove in his yellow-gloved hand. Dan had worked for him for a fortnight, and was learning to keep a special boyish grin for the chairmen of the various committees, to create an attitude rarely cringing, yet always sufficiently deferential.

"I wonder, Graveson, whether you could take the minutes for the AOs tonight?" Spencer asked.

His tone of voice implied: although I speak jauntily, this, young man, is your chance to prove yourself.

Dan's navy suit and blue-and-gold old school tie contrasted with the virgin whiteness and special glossiness of a brand-new Van Heusen collar, style eleven. He travelled by taxi to the Mayfair address. A pretty starched white-and-bright-blue maid opened the fine front door:

"May I take your coat, sir? The AO meeting is in the front lounge, sir. Thank you, sir. This way, sir."

Three chaps in middle-aged sports jackets sipped sherry together. Dan stood close to the wall, holding the cardboard file Spencer had given him. He walked over to the table, took a glass of sherry from the silver tray, felt himself in the middle of the room.

More people came: ladies with expensive legs, company directors who looked like company directors, talking together of maids and motor cars.

"Mr Graveson?"

The hostess beckoned to him.

"Have you everything you need? A pen? Do use this card table for your papers."

Like a Jane Austen curate, he sat straightening his papers, while the guests finished their sherry and slowly settled elegant bottoms in elegant chairs.

In a cultured voice Dan read the minutes of the last meeting, at which it had been decided that the ninth annual AO ball should be held at the Saveloy Hotel. The meeting then proceeded to the discussion of the main item on the agenda: the question of prizes for the tombola. The chairman of a whisky firm offered a case of whisky as first prize. He was congratulated, thanked, held up as an example. "Simply splendid," said the treasurer; "if we had a few more Gerald Felthams all our problems would be solved."

The price of tombola tickets was debated passionately. Finally a compromise motion, referring the matter back for decision by the annual-ball tombola subcommittee, was carried by eighteen votes to nine with eleven abstentions. The treasurer estimated that the tombola should make approximately two hundred pounds profit.

"What's that in terms of AOs?" he asked Dan.

Dan read from the illustrated leaflet:

"Two and sixpence will buy enough dried milk to maintain an Asian orphan in good health for approximately five days."

"Simply splendid," the treasurer said.

Dan didn't go to Spencer's office the next morning, or ever again. Spencer wrote, at first politely, then rudely, asking for the return of his AO file.

Chapter 8

MULTILITH OPERATOR, Adrema embosser, accounts clerk, upholsterer, Burroughs P600 operator, invoice checker, delivery man, marine engineer, capstan-lathe operator, warehouseman, stove enameller, reinforced-concrete engineer, window dresser, pig man. He was none of these. He wasn't even a hairdresser's assistant. Two columns of vacancies for shorthand typists. He bought a *Teach Yourself Shorthand* book, explained to the landlady that, as soon as he got through it, say twenty-four hours' solid work, he would be earning at least ten pounds a week. He reached chapter three.

He was thrown out of his room. Bodily. There's the rent and the state you leave your room in it's not nice the smell and tins everywhere the bed unmade dust all over sink blocked up it's not nice for the other tenants not that they've complained but it's not nice.

Be out by morning. He wasn't. Her brother came. Headbutting bastard. Armwrenched body-buffeted buttockbumped bullied and socked downstairs and out.

Bums in lines queued for jobs and thirty-bob-odd doled out by clerks from behind heavy wire.

"Report three times a week to get your card stamped."

To make sure you've not got a job same time as you're collecting. Dan waited all morning between tough blokes – Irish and Jamaican. Didn't talk to them. Shuffled up as queue moved forwards. One bloke bounced on his toes, swinging a violin case so that everyone knew he was not an ordinary bum but a musical bum.

By hungry lunchtime Dan found out he was in the manual-labour queue. Bricklayer's assistants only.

"All right, I'll take that."

"No, son, you've got school certificate. Come next Thursday – ask for the clerical department."

He walked down streets, strange ones. Camden Town. He sat on a seat placed on a triangle of grass between busy roads. Good to sit down, lots to look at. Bless the Victorian philanthropist. Then women carrying shopping gooped at him.

Parkwandering, somewhere, he set a deckchair on its feet, wiped the birdshit off, sat. Got up, altered the back strut, sat again, more stretched out, nearer the ground. An attendant tinged close by. He leapt up, sat on a wooden seat, a free one. Nowhere to sleep. Lucky it was warm.

He went to the free lavatory. The door was lower than the penny lavs. He moved with bent knees so that his head should not be seen. A spade and two brooms were kept there. One broom soft for dust, the other thick copper, red spines wet with disinfectant. No pick-up seat; only a rim of stained wood. Advertisements for venereal diseases. A metal notice above an empty box: "Toilet paper must be obtained from the attendant". A tramp with dirty bum must hobble out and ask for paper, please.

He found a sheltered place to sleep, protected from the slight evening wind. He took off his jacket, bunched it into a pillow, lay his cheek on it. Shivered. Picked up a fallen log for a pillow. Beetles. Flung it away. Stood still. Bells rang ArangArangArang.

"A-a-a-a-l Out! A-a-a-a-a-a-l Out!"

Hide. Down quick on his knees in the leaves, heart bumping. No. He got up, brushed the earth off his clothes, ambled out of the main gate. It was damp and cold now.

Raw noise. Tens of thousands of wheels on roads. Heaps of persons, hives of them, pouring from and into buildings, crowding up steps from underground, crouching in cars, stopping up the street gaping at gadgets in windows, getting pinched elbowed killed drunk dazed, reading evening papers, obeying police-men, selling (and buying) fruit. He bored through them, out to Holborn and the dead City where the daytime money-magnet was switched off, and it was empty. Greenish light lay on the windows of banks, insurance houses, tobacconists. Policemen shone square lights at doors and tested locks.

Blitz sites. He was walking with conscious leverage from leg to leg. His legs weighed impossibly heavy. He came to a thudding hellplace, gleams of fires, men swung shovels, the ground shook, it was between mountains.

"What's happening?"

"Government contract. Double shifts."

The steepening road grew bendier, slummier. Tramlines whipped away, shining. He looked at the headlamps of cars spinning round roadbends, coming and going, like spies signalling, but not to him. Asphalt now, to fall and cut your knee on. Everyone's got a scar on his knee from falling off a bicycle or something, onto a gritty road; an inch of blue-grey dead. The regular street lights passed him one to the other. He was lit by two lights making two faint shadows; the third substantial shadow where the two overlapped had an unhuman shape. Tremendous lorries bound for Glasgow, Strasbourg, Benghazi thundered past him onwards, paralysing as panzer divisions. A dog barked. Bing beng, quarter past something. He found a nameless place with smashed windows and swinging door and a man on a backless chair. He crept in, lay on the floor, felt his head and spine against stone. His feet swing high and round and round in gorges, canyons.

Slammed in the ribs by boulders:

"Out you get, out of it. Railway's property. Out with you. Come on, out of it."

Very slowly the morning sun warmed him. It was going to be another fine day. He stood with his back to a lamppost, turned his face into the sun for a moment. He'd ended up at Billingsgate, of all places. The insane fish smell drove him up the hill, spitting. He passed a dead bus stuck in a hole, and early workers whistling. "Ullo Ken, 'ow yer goin'?"

"Can't complain."

He had been here before, ages ago, with his father. He found a halfpenny on the pavement. A kid pointed at his shoe: "Look mum, it's got its mouth open."

Policemen glanced at him.

He finished the tea and the ham roll and walked slowly to the door.

"Not so fast. That's tenpence."

"So sorry. I clean forgot."

He felt in his trouser pockets. Halfpenny. He looked intently into his wallet. An old woman pushed in, past him. A wrinkled stick from an Irish hedge, crimson hair tangling from under her hat, which had berries on it. She hooked her man's umbrella onto the counter, and in a sharp Belfast voice asked for a cup of tea. But the man looked past her:

"Well?"

"I haven't a penny on me," Dan called from the door, keeping his grip on the handle. "Now what do we do? I'm really most dreadfully sorry. A cheque for tenpence, of course, would be ridiculous."

"Buzz off. Go on, get moving. And don't come this way again in a hurry. I'll know your mug for next time."

He had to get decent. He got back to his father's home, knowing his father would be at work in the afternoon. Helen came to the door, wiping her hands on her apron.

"Dan! What a state you're in! So that's how you've been carrying on. I thought you were meant to be studying."

"I'd like some lunch, please."

"It's half-past three. Nearly teatime."

He shoved past her into the kitchen. She followed, stood holding the door. He opened the fridge, took out a bottle of milk, a cold roast chicken, a carton of potato salad.

"That's your father's supper."

"He'll understand."

"But there's nothing else in the house. What am I going to tell him? What will he say?"

They stood over him.

Note on the Text

The text in the present edition is based on that in the first edition of *New Writers 1*, published by John Calder (Publishers) Ltd, 1961. The spelling and punctuation in the text have been standardized, modernized and made consistent throughout, with the exception of words deliberately run together by Burns, which have been retained.

The unusual formatting in the text – the non-indentation of paragraphs – has been replicated from the first edition in order to follow the author's wishes as closely as possible, preserving the aleatoric device and his professed wish to "cock a snook at the body of traditional literature".

Notes

p. 9, *Mr Chamberlain*: Neville Chamberlain (1869–1940) was Prime Minister of the United Kingdom from 1937 until his death in 1940; he gave a memorable speech, which is alluded to here, saying "this country is at war with Germany", which marked the beginning of the Second World War.

p. 14, *'The Marseillaise'... Republic*: 'La Marseillaise', now the national anthem of France, was a rallying call during the French Revolution.

p. 18, *War and Peace... Pierre*: Count Pyotr Kirillovich ("Pierre" Bezukhov) is the central character in Leo Tolstoy's (1828–1910) novel *War and Peace* (1869).

p. 18, *Seccotine*: A brand of glue.

p. 19, *Hooper coachwork*: Hooper & Co. was a London coachbuilder.

p. 22, *Left Book Club, Thinker's Library*: The Left Book Club was a subscription-based publisher with strong left-wing leanings. Thinker's Library was a series of essays and extracts from greater works.

p. 23, *Radio Malt*: A brand of malt extract.

p. 24, *Lasker and Capablanca*: Emanuel Lasker (1868–1941) and José Raúl Capablanca (1888–1942) were famous chess players.

p. 25, *"Quel sang froid! Quel savoir-faire!*: "What cold blood! What manners!" (French).

p. 26, *Tom Paine*: Thomas Paine (1737–1809) was an English-American philosopher, and the author of the influential treatise *Rights of Man* (1791).

p. 26, *Johnson in the Modern Eye*: This essay was allegedly written by Burns, aged sixteen, and published in the school magazine.

p. 30, *NAAFI*: An acronym for the Navy, Army and Air Force Institutes.

p. 32, *CO*: Commanding Officer.

p. 34, *CB... fatigues*: "CB" means "Confined to barracks"; "fatigues" are menial tasks doled out as punishment.

p. 35, *Civvy Street*: Civilian life. In this instance, life before joining the forces.

p. 35, *Queens Regulations*: A set of rules and regulations governing the personal conduct of officers in the armed forces.

p. 36, *blanco*: To treat with blanco, a preparation used for whitening.

p. 55, *Lenin on Imperialist War*: A reference to 'Turn Imperialist War into Civil War', a 1915 pamphlet written by Lenin and Grigory Zinoviev (1883–1936).

p. 62, *DJ*: Dinner jacket.

p. 65, *RSMs*: Regimental sergeant majors.

p. 66, *the twenty-five-pounders*: The British army's primary artillery field gun during the Second World War.

p. 66, *Audi alteram partem*: "Listen to the other side" (Latin) – the principle that no one should be judged without being given a fair hearing.

p. 70, *NCOs*: Non-commissioned officers.

p. 70, *Pte.*: Private.

p. 79, *Danny Kaye*: Danny Kaye (1911–87) was an American actor.

p. 80, *MacArthur*: Douglas MacArthur (1880–1964) was the General of the US Army.

p. 93, *the Garden*: Covent Garden market.

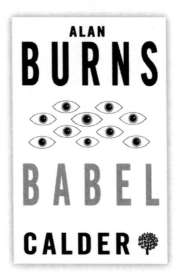

Babel contains all the hallmarks of the aleatoric style Burns helped to define.

By turns comic and tragic, tender and brutal, religious and blasphemous, the narrative rockets from London to the United States to Vietnam to interstellar space, familiar events are constantly fragmented and reset into new patterns, and ultimately *Babel* becomes a cautionary tale about the tragedy arising from attempting to build Utopia.

Celebrations brings the inherent violence and oppression so apparent in *Europe after the Rain* into the setting of a family-owned factory.

By bringing the differences between workers sharply into focus, Burns creates a choking atmosphere of oppression and exploitation – heightened and upended by his trademark aleatoric style, peppering with seemingly random headlines and offcuts the text, which has not lost any of either its relevance or its acerbic bite in the intervening years.

BY THE SAME AUTHOR

DREAMERIKA!

Dreamerika!, Alan Burns's fourth novel, first published in 1972, provides a satirical look at the Kennedy political dynasty.

Presented in a fragmented form that reflects society's disintegration, *Dreamerika!* fuses fact and dream, resulting in a surreal biography, an alternate history which lays bare the corruption and excesses of capitalism just as the heady idealism of the 1960s has begun to fade.

Europe after the Rain takes its title from Max Ernst's surrealist work, which depicts a vision of rampant destruction – a theme which Burns here takes to its conclusion.

The Europe through which the unnamed narrator travels is a devastated world, twisted and misshapen, both geographically and morally, and he is forced to witness terrible sights, to which he brings an interested apathy, without ever succumbing to despair or cynicism.

CALDER PUBLICATIONS

EDGY TITLES FROM A LEGENDARY LIST

Heliogabalus,
or The Anarchist Crowned
Antonin Artaud

Babel
Alan Burns

Buster
Alan Burns

Celebrations
Alan Burns

Dreamerika!
Alan Burns

Europe after the Rain
Alan Burns

Changing Track
Michel Butor

Moderato Cantabile
Marguerite Duras

The Garden Square
Marguerite Duras